Jarrett studied the unconscious woman.

Long blond hair fanned out on the sand. She wore a one-piece swimsuit and shorts. No shoes. Mid-twenties, pretty. He'd never seen her before in his life.

Giving in to the inevitable, Jarrett scooped up the mysterious stranger in his arms and carried her back to the house. A soft moan escaped from her lips. The woman's eyes fluttered, then opened. Her irises were the color of summer grass. Pure green. She blinked.

She glanced around the room. "Where am I?"

"In my private residence," Jarrett said. "You've had a little accident in the ocean, but you're okay now. I almost forgot to ask your name."

"I'm—" She paused, mouth open. Her lips moved, but no sound emerged. The smile faded and her eyes widened slightly. Fingers fluttered as her hand reached out into the air.

She looked defeated. "I don't know my name...."

Dear Reader,

Fall is to be savored for all its breathtaking glory—and a spectacular October lineup awaits at Special Edition!

For years, readers have treasured Tracy Sinclair's captivating romances...and October commemorates her fiftieth Silhouette book! To help celebrate this wonderful author's crowning achievement, be sure to check out *The Princess Gets Engaged*— an enthralling romance that finds American tourist Megan Delaney in a royal mess when she masquerades as a princess and falls hopelessly in love with the charming Prince Nicholas.

This month's THAT'S MY BABY! title is by Lois Faye Dyer. *He's Got His Daddy's Eyes* is a poignant reunion story about hope, the enduring power of love and how one little boy works wonders on two broken hearts.

Nonstop romance continues as three veteran authors deliver enchanting stories. Check out award-winning author Marie Ferrarella's adorable tale about mismatched lovers when a blue-blooded heroine hastily marries a blue-collar carpenter in *Wanted: Husband, Will Train*. And what's an amnesiac triplet to do when she washes up on shore and right into the arms of a brooding billionaire? Find out in *The Mysterious Stranger*, when Susan Mallery's engaging TRIPLE TROUBLE series splashes to a finish! Reader favorite Arlene James serves up a tender story about unexpected love in *The Knight, The Waitress and the Toddler*— book four in our FROM BUD TO BLOSSOM promo series.

Finally, October's WOMAN TO WATCH is debut author Lisette Belisle, who unfolds an endearing romance between an innocent country girl and a gruff drifter in *Just Jessie*.

I hope you enjoy these books, and all of the stories to come!

Sincerely,

Tara Gavin, Senior Editor

Please address questions and book requests to:
Silhouette Reader Service
U.S.: 3010 Walden Ave., P.O. Box 1325, Buffalo, NY 14269
Canadian: P.O. Box 609, Fort Erie, Ont. L2A 5X3

SUSAN MALLERY
THE MYSTERIOUS STRANGER

SPECIAL EDITION®

Published by Silhouette Books

America's Publisher of Contemporary Romance

To Mike, who appeared unexpectedly in my life.
You've made me believe that the fantasy of romance,
true love and happily ever after can be real. May we
always find the magic in each other's eyes.

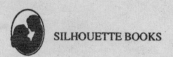

SILHOUETTE BOOKS

ISBN 0-373-24130-5

THE MYSTERIOUS STRANGER

Copyright © 1997 by Susan W. Macias

Printed in U.S.A.

Books by Susan Mallery

Silhouette Special Edition

Tender Loving Care #717
More Than Friends #802
A Dad for Billie #834
Cowboy Daddy #898
*The Best Bride #933
*Marriage on Demand #939
*Father in Training #969
The Bodyguard & Ms. Jones #1008
*Part-Time Wife #1027
Full-Time Father #1042
*Holly and Mistletoe #1071
*Husband by the Hour #1099
†The Girl of His Dreams #1118
†The Secret Wife #1123
†The Mysterious Stranger #1130

*Hometown Heartbreakers
†Triple Trouble

Silhouette Intimate Moments

Tempting Faith #554
The Only Way Out #646
Surrender in Silk #770

SUSAN MALLERY

lives in sunny Southern California where the eccentricities of a writer are considered fairly normal. Her books are both reader favorites and bestsellers, with titles appearing on the Waldenbooks' bestseller list and the *USA Today* bestseller list. Her 1995 Special Edition *Marriage on Demand* was awarded "Best Special Edition" by *Romantic Times* magazine.

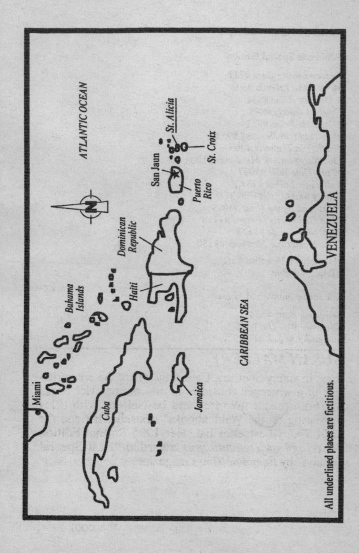

ATLANTIC OCEAN

Miami

Bahama
Islands

N

Cuba

Haiti

Dominican
Republic

San Jaun

St. Alicia

Puerto
Rico

St. Croix

Jamaica

CARIBBEAN SEA

VENEZUELA

All underlined places are fictitious.

Prologue

Anna Jane touched the smooth wood of the study doors and sighed softly. She loved her uncle Jarrett. She knew she was a lucky girl to have someone to take care of her after her mother died. But sometimes she wished he didn't try so hard to be her guardian. She wished it was easy for him to be with her and love her. She wished he could be her friend as well as a grown-up.

But he was busy, she reminded herself. Too busy. Uncle Jarrett had an empire to run. At least, that's what her mother had always said when she'd talked about him.

"Uncle Jarrett was born to run the world, Anna Jane. That's why he's not coming for Christmas." Or her birthday, or even her mother's birthday. Uncle Jarrett had responsibilities, many of which were more important than one nine-year-old girl.

Anna Jane walked away from the study and headed up the stairs. Her sandals slapped against the cool marble flooring, the sounds coming closer and closer together as she raced to the second floor. Climbing the stairs made her nervous. The house was so big and so quiet. Sometimes she felt there were creatures ready to nip at her heels if she didn't hurry.

She didn't tell her uncle about her fears because she didn't think he would understand. Men who ran empires probably didn't worry about imaginary creatures nipping at anything.

She reached her room and closed the door behind her. The bedroom had been decorated with her comfort in mind. Swags of pale pink fabric hung over the canopy. Light-colored furniture filled the walls. She had a dresser, a desk, bookshelves and a big storage unit for her toys. Her clothes didn't fill even a quarter of the rack space in the closet. Yet, in here, with the world shut out, she felt safe.

She crossed to the window and stared out at the deep blue of the Caribbean Sea. Waves rolled onto the shore. She liked the water and the beach, although she wasn't allowed to go down to the ocean by herself. She liked the smells of the island, the warm sun, even though it was December. Sometimes she remembered that it would be snowing back home in New York. When she remembered, she missed her friends, her old room and Nana B.

Anna Jane squeezed her eyes tightly shut so she wouldn't cry. Babies cried; she was nearly grown up. But it was hard to fight the loneliness. If only she had a friend here on the island. Someone she could play with and talk to. Someone to give her hugs and maybe even remember that Christmas was in two weeks. She didn't think Uncle Jarrett was going to remember on his own, and she hadn't figured out a way to remind him.

When the threat of tears faded, she opened her eyes

and glanced around her room. Maybe she would feel better if she read a book. She walked to the shelves and looked at the pile of new stories. Nothing caught her attention and she found herself tracing the spines of books she'd already read. They weren't exactly like having someone to talk to, but they were old friends who often kept her company. Her finger paused by a familiar title. She remembered that story. A young girl was held captive in a faraway land. She sent a message in a bottle, asking someone to help her escape.

Anna Jane smiled. Maybe she could do the same thing—send a message in a bottle and ask for a friend.

She hurried to her desk and quickly wrote a brief note. On the back she drew a rough outline of the island and put an *X* on the spot that marked the house. In her bathroom she studied the bottles of bath salts, picking up one before setting it down and reaching for the bottle on the end.

The container was tall and beautifully shaped, like a series of graduated bubbles sitting on top of each other. The bubbles were large at the bottom and got smaller and smaller toward the top. She pulled open the cork top and dumped the contents into a glass, then rolled the paper in a long cylinder and dropped it inside. She secured the cork in place and raced for the stairs.

Once at the front door, Anna Jane frowned. Though she wasn't allowed down at the beach by herself, she didn't want anyone else knowing about her bottle, either. Besides, the waves might push the glass up against the rocks and break it. There was a shallow pond that fed a stream on the far side of the house. She could let her bottle go there.

Ten minutes later Anna Jane watched her bottle bobbing in the water. It flowed with the slow current, lazily moving toward the bend that would take it out of sight. She clenched her hands tightly together and sent up a prayer that someone would find her note and want to be her friend....

Chapter One

Fallon Bedford stretched out on the lounge chair in front of her bungalow and tried to tell herself she was having a great time. The lie didn't sit well on her usually clean conscience. The truth was, paradise for one wasn't all she'd hoped it would be.

"You're on vacation," she told herself. "Relax."

The command didn't have a soothing effect. She pushed her sunglasses up on her nose and took a deep breath. The sun was warm on her skin, the sky was an impossibly vivid shade of blue. Next to her on the small table sat a fashion magazine and a tropical drink heavily laced with rum. Her goal had been to enjoy herself the entire day and not worry about anything. She'd made it all the way to 1:30 in the afternoon before boredom had struck.

Maybe it had been a mistake to come to the island so early. It had seemed like a good idea at the time. An odd quirk in the school calendar had ended the semester a full two weeks before Christmas. Rather than sit at home until her sisters and their husbands were ready to start their holiday vacation, she'd decided to strike out early. The bungalow they'd reserved had been available, so she'd simply moved up the reservation and flown out by herself. She had ten days alone to sun, surf and do whatever else people did in places like this.

Unfortunately it was 1:30 on day one, and she was already restless.

"You're an ingrate," she said out loud as she sat up. "Or maybe just not used to having free time." The fifth graders kept her busy. Between the demands of her job, staying in touch with her two sisters and planning for her future, she hadn't had much down time. In a couple of days it would be easier to do nothing. But for now she needed to give in to the antsy feeling and take a walk.

Fallon collected the brightly colored wrap that matched her bathing suit and tied it around her waist. The soft fabric fell to the middle of her calves. She grabbed her hat and room key, took a last sip of her drink, then headed for the path that would lead to the main hotel.

The resort was a combination of romantic getaway and tropical heaven. Although the Wilkenson hotel chain was known for exceptional facilities, here on the island of St. Alicia they'd outdone themselves.

Individual bungalows surrounded a five-acre lagoon at the east side of the property. The hotel itself was built in three wings, stretching nearly a half mile from end to end. The beach wrapped around the island, a string of white sand and private coves all outlined by warm blue water. Fallon had heard rumors that it was possible to circumnavigate the island by heading in one direction or the other on the beach. She'd decided against putting that rumor to the test. For one thing, St. Alicia was over five hundred square miles, and she had no desire to walk that far, at least not in her sandals.

A path wound around the lagoon, the smooth stones going right to the water's edge. She strolled slowly, breathing in the tropical sweetness lacing the air. Birds called to each other as they darted from tree to tree. Bright flowers dotted the bushes and vines along the path. Little lizards dozed in shady spots on rocks.

As she rounded the curve in the lagoon, something in the water caught her attention. At first she thought it was a fish, but the shape was wrong and whatever it was didn't disappear under the surface. She moved closer, bent and pulled out a glass bottle. Inside was a rolled piece of paper.

Fallon glanced around, half wondering if someone was playing a trick on her. A note in a bottle? Surely that didn't happen in real life. Yet here it was. She moved to one of the stone benches set up around the path and sank onto the smooth, warm seat. After wiggling the cork free, she shook out the note, then spread it flat.

"My name is Anna Jane, and I'm nine years old. I live in a big house on the north end of the island. I don't have anyone to play with. If you find this note, I hope you'll come visit me and be my friend."

At the bottom of the page was the word *over.* Fallon obediently turned the sheet and saw a hand drawn map with an *X* marking the little girl's house.

"How sad," Fallon murmured. While her family hadn't been perfect, at least she'd been fortunate enough to grow up with two sisters who cared about her. Other children weren't that lucky. In her classes she had some students who had been abandoned by loved ones. A divorce that forced one parent to leave, the death of a sibling, young mothers who could barely take care of themselves, let alone a child.

She studied the map. The shape of the island definitely looked like St. Alicia, so the house must be here, too. Maybe it wasn't too far away. If the parents didn't mind, she would like to visit this lonely little girl. They could help each other fill the time.

She took the paper with her as she made her way to the main hotel. Out by the pool was a long bar with a thatch awning. She took one of the stools and smiled when the bartender came to take her order.

She glanced at his name tag. "Joshua," she said, putting the map on the bar and turning it toward him, "do you know where this house is?"

The man was in his early twenties, with dark good looks that probably tempted a fair number of the female guests. He studied the crude drawing. "It looks like the big house," he said. "Mr. Wilkenson lives there."

"The owner of the resort?"

Joshua nodded.

"So his daughter must have sent this," she said, more to herself than the bartender. "Where's his wife?"

Joshua frowned. "No wife. Mr. Wilkenson isn't married. There's no little girl, either."

"But there must be." She turned over the note and tapped it. "She wrote this."

Joshua scanned the page. "I don't know who she is."

"How odd." This really wasn't any of her business, Fallon reminded herself. But she didn't have anything else to do, and the girl sounded as if she really needed a friend. "Is there another house near Mr. Wilkenson's property? Maybe they're the ones with the child."

"The boss doesn't have any neighbors. You could find his place easy. Follow the beach north about four miles.

You'll know it when you see it. Be warned, Mr. Wilkenson doesn't like company.''

"I'm not surprised." The owner of the resort and the famous Wilkenson hotel chain was rumored to be a recluse. "I'm not interested in the man, just the little girl, if she even exists. Don't worry. I won't tell him you gave me directions.''

Joshua leaned toward her and smiled. "Good. I don't want to have to go talk to Mr. Wilkenson. My shift is over in two hours and I'm going home for the holidays.''

"Where's home?"

"Jamaica. I have five sisters and three brothers. This is our first Christmas together in four years." He glanced at his watch. "The plane leaves at five.''

She slid off her stool. "When I see it fly overhead, I'll wave." She held the piece of paper. "Have a great holiday, Joshua. And thanks for the information.''

He gave her a smile, then turned toward a young couple stepping up to the bar.

Fallon studied the map. Four miles walking along the beach was going to be like a six-mile hike on a path. Sand was a killer. "Think of what it will do for your thighs," she told herself, and glanced up at the sky. It was nearly two. There was no way to find the house and get back in the remaining daylight. She would rather not have to count on Jarrett Wilkenson's hospitality for the night. She would go in the morning. She could get to the house, find out if there was a lonely little girl there or not, and be back at the hotel by sundown.

Having a plan and something to do lightened her spirits considerably. She circled the pool, nodding at the couples spread out there. For the first time since she'd arrived, she didn't feel quite so alone.

* * *

Fallon made an early start the next morning. Along with her breakfast, she'd had room service deliver a box lunch and a couple of bottles of water. She put the food in an old canvas tote, along with sunscreen and a towel.

She pulled the door firmly shut behind her and checked to make sure it was locked. Then she headed out to the beach. It was barely after eight and the soft white sand was deserted except for a few diehard joggers at the water's edge. Fallon didn't feel any need to join them. If she made it to the house and back, she would have gone eight miles. That was enough exercise for anyone.

Waves rolled in to the shore. The rhythmic sound soothed her. She adjusted the wide-brimmed wicker hat she wore and smiled. No matter the outcome of her journey, she was glad she'd decided to make it. She'd spent the past several months in a classroom with twenty-eight bright, active ten-year-olds. She needed a break.

Three hours later Fallon's easy stride had turned into a ragged stumble. Her thighs ached from the constant pull of the fine sand. She'd worn athletic shoes in case she had to climb over anything, but except for the twenty-foot sheer cliff on her right, there weren't rocks on St. Alicia. There wasn't anything but sun, sand and water. Endless sea that stretched out to eternity. And who knew the sun could be so hot?

Fallon pulled off her hat and waved it in front of her face. If the heat on her cheeks and shoulders was anything to go by, SPF 30 sunscreen hadn't been enough to keep her pale skin from burning. In the past two hours she hadn't seen another living soul, nor any signs that the area was indeed inhabited. If she hadn't actually spent a couple of nights at a beautiful resort, she would have sworn she'd been dropped onto a deserted island by mistake.

"You would have made a lousy navy SEAL," she told herself as she plopped down on the sand. She settled her hat back on her head and thought longingly of shade. Lovely, cool shade. There was plenty to be had...in the lush riot of vegetation she'd left behind at the hotel. Just none here.

"A lousy navy SEAL and not much of an adventuress," she said, digging in her tote bag for a water bottle. She'd finished the first one and was halfway through a second. San Francisco winter hadn't prepared her for the heat of the tropics. It might be December on the calendar, but no one had told the sun beating down on her.

She wiped her sweaty face on her towel, then opened her box lunch. There were few problems in life that couldn't be aided by a sandwich or some cookies.

When she'd finished her meal, she spread out her map and wondered how far she'd come. Joshua had said the main house was only four miles. She must be close. If only Anna Jane had thought to draw the map to scale.

Fallon grinned at the thought, then sighed sleepily. It was the heat, she knew. She was feeling a little light-headed. Maybe she should just close her eyes for a minute.

She tucked the letter in her pocket, stretched out on the sand and used her hat to cover her face. Within seconds she was drifting off, almost asleep but faintly aware of the passage of time. Something soft and comforting cradled her, lifting her up, higher and higher. She drew in a deep breath—

And came up choking.

Fallon's eyes popped open. Something was terribly wrong. Her mind took precious seconds to clear, and all the while she struggled to catch her breath, to clear her lungs, to breathe! She stared around in horror as she realized the tide had come in to the sheltered cove and she was at risk of drowning. The water was up to the cliff, covering the entire beach.

Stay calm, she told herself. She tried to relax, to let herself float. Everything was going to be fine. She could swim. It was just the tide. The cove wasn't that big. If she had to, she would swim in the direction of the resort, and eventually she would come to the beach where she'd been walking and be able to make shore. It wasn't that far.

When her panic faded to a manageable level, she rolled onto her stomach and started swimming back the way she'd come. She worked at an angle, heading close to the cliffs in hopes of being able to touch bottom. The water didn't look as deep there.

Her long hair swirled around her face and she brushed it away. When her feet felt heavy, she kicked off her shoes. She'd nearly reached the cliff wall when the first cramp struck.

The pain shocked her and she doubled over in distress. As she gasped, she swallowed a mouthful of water and started to choke. With the second cramp, panic returned and Fallon started to cry. She coughed and held her side, all the while struggling to stay afloat in the warm sea.

A wave broke over her, pushing her toward the cliff. The rocky walls loomed closer. She kicked away from them and managed to draw a clean breath. Then her stomach convulsed again. The next wave pushed her nearer to the unforgiving stone. She held out her hand to brace herself but it wasn't enough. The last thing she remembered was the searing impact of slamming into the rigid, vertical surface.

"Tell them the bid is final," Jarrett Wilkenson said, turning his back on the spectacular view exposed by the floor-to-ceiling glass windows in his office. "Either they sign or we walk away. Understood?"

"Yes, sir," the voice on the other end of the phone replied briskly. "Just two more items on the agenda."

Jarrett pulled a sheet of paper toward him and crossed off the third-last line. These biweekly conference calls took a lot of time, but they were easier than flying back to the States and meeting with everyone in person.

"There is still the matter of the Riverbend hotel," his caller said. "According to my sources..."

The door to Jarrett's office flew open. Anna Jane dashed into the room. "Uncle Jarrett, come quick! There's an emergency."

He glanced at his niece. Her dark eyes were wide with fear.

"Hold on, Roberts," he said, and pressed the Mute button. "What is it?" he asked the girl.

She skittered to a stop in front of his desk and pressed her hands tightly together. "There's a lady on the beach," she said quickly. "Frank said she probably got caught in the cove and washed ashore. She's hurt. He says she needs a doctor."

Jarrett nodded. He released the Mute button and spoke.

"We'll pick this up later, Roberts. I have to take care of something here." He hung up without waiting for a reply. By pressing two different buttons, he engaged his autodialer. When a woman answered the phone, he explained about the injured person on the beach and received confirmation the doctor would be sent right away.

He rose to his feet and started for the door. A mysterious woman washing up on his beach. He grimaced. It was a good trick—original, if risky. But they were often willing to take incredible risks to get to him. Somehow he'd thought he would be safe here. For a while he had been.

He crossed the foyer of the large house and headed for the rear doors. From there it was a short walk to the beach.

The woman had probably made her way up from the resort. Had she known about the danger of high tide in the cove? Had she counted on it? Or hadn't she noticed the watermarks on the stony cliffs?

It didn't matter, he told himself. As soon as the doctor arrived, the woman could be transported back wherever she belonged. If he was smart, he wouldn't even risk meeting her. Yet he couldn't stay away. He had to see her face. He had to make sure she was alive.

"Uncle Jarrett?" The breathless call from behind him reminded him he'd left Anna Jane in his office. He slowed his long stride and waited for the girl to catch up. She trotted toward him and raised her small, stubborn chin until she could see his face. "Uncle Jarrett, I think I did a bad thing."

Her lower lip trembled at the admission. At times he could see traces of his sister in Anna Jane's face. Shadows of familiar expressions, words spoken in a certain tone or cadence that took him back to a nearly forgotten past. But other times, his niece was a stranger. Perhaps because he'd seen her only half a dozen times in her young life. Until he'd brought her here after her mother's funeral a few weeks ago, they'd never been alone together.

A bad thing? What did that mean? What did he know of children and their faults? Tracy should have named someone else as the girl's guardian. A friend with children of her own. Someone who knew what to do when faced with big eyes and a confession of wrongdoing.

"I see," he said.

Anna Jane nodded. "I didn't mean to. I was lonely and I wanted someone to play with so I wrote a letter."

"That's hardly bad," he said, turning away and starting for the beach.

"There's more."

He paused and glanced back at her. The path angled down to the beach. Anna Jane stood at the crest of the rise, a small figure dwarfed by the large trees and the three-story house behind her. He heard her words for the first time. *I was lonely.*

Loneliness was a familiar companion in his world. He'd grown to accept it as one accepts a chronic pain or an annoying relative who has decided to move in. Yet he hadn't thought about a child being lonely. Weren't children always going and doing? Again he wondered what Tracy had been thinking when she'd written her will. Then he reminded himself his sister had not expected to die so young.

He stared at the forlorn little girl and wished he could do better for her.

"I asked whoever got the letter to come visit me," Anna Jane continued. "I drew a map of the island and marked the house."

"I don't see what—"

"I put the letter in a bottle, then sent it out in the water," she interrupted. "That's why she came. She found my letter and now she's going to die."

Like Mommy. Anna Jane didn't say the words, but Jarrett heard them. Loneliness and guilt. A pair of hounds that guarded the gates of hell. How would he explain that none of this was her fault?

"If you put your bottle in the ocean recently, it wouldn't have had time to get to another island," he said.

Her hands twisted together as she considered the information, then she smiled. "You're right. I just sent the bottle yesterday." She walked to his side and touched his arm. "Thanks, Uncle Jarrett."

"No problem. Let's go check on our mystery guest."

He led the way down to the beach. Frank and Leona, the married couple who acted as housekeeper and head gardener for the estate, crouched beside a still figure on the sand.

"Stay here," he told Anna Jane, then crossed the last twenty feet to the woman.

Leona stood as he approached. "Oh, Mr. Jarrett, Anna Jane told you about her. Poor thing." She motioned to the woman. "She's breathing, but she won't wake up. Frank says there's no way to tell what's wrong. Did you call the doctor? Do you know who she is? One of the guests, perhaps. Or someone on a day sail. She could have fallen off her boat."

Leona continued to list an assortment of possible fates, all of which ended badly. Jarrett knelt next to the woman and pressed his fingers against her neck. A faint pulse thudded steadily.

"You know her?" he asked his gardener, suspecting the answer in advance.

"No."

Jarrett studied the still figure. Except for the dark bruise on the left side of her face, a gash on her forehead and the scratches on her arms and legs, she was pale. Long blond hair fanned out on the sand. She wore a one-piece swimsuit and shorts. No shoes. Mid-twenties, pretty. He'd never seen her before in his life.

"I don't think anything is broken," Frank said.

"Good."

Giving in to the inevitable, Jarrett scooped the unconscious woman up in his arms and carried her back to the house. By the time he'd placed her in one of the guest bedrooms, Dr. John Reed had arrived. Leona showed him upstairs, and Jarrett met him in the doorway.

The two men shook hands. John had graduated from a prestigious medical school and gone into a high-volume, lucrative practice in New York. After fifteen years he'd been close to burning out. Jarrett had offered him tropical paradise, a waterfront home and enough money to enjoy his new life. The island had its first resident doctor and John Reed had avoided leaving medicine altogether.

"What's going on?" the older man asked as he approached the woman lying on the bed.

Jarrett filled him in with what he knew. He sensed Leona, Frank and Anna Jane hovering in the doorway.

"She's young," John said. "Pretty, too."

"Uh-huh." Jarrett couldn't have been less interested.

John examined her. "Nothing broken. Just scrapes. She probably swallowed a lot of water. I—"

A soft moan cut him off. Jarrett moved closer to the bed. The woman's eyes fluttered, then opened. Her irises were the color of summer grass. Pure green. She blinked.

"What—" She broke off and coughed.

John sat on the bed next to her and smiled. "Don't worry, you're fine. You had a little accident in the ocean, but you're okay now. I'm Dr. John Reed. Take a deep breath before you try to talk."

The woman did as she was instructed. "I was in the ocean?" she asked. She glanced around the room. "Where am I?"

"In a private residence," John said. "How do you feel?"

The woman shifted, then winced. "Sore, but okay."

She reached up and touched her face. "Did I hit something?"

"It looks that way." John shone a penlight into her eyes. "How many fingers am I holding up?"

"Two," the woman said. "I'm not dizzy, if that's what you're trying to find out. The room's not spinning or anything. My stomach's a little upset and I feel shaken, but not badly injured."

"Good." He glanced at Jarrett. "I'd like to keep her quiet for the next day or so before moving her, but I think she's going to be fine."

Jarrett swallowed his instinctive refusal. John knew enough about his past that he wouldn't ask if he didn't think it was important. "Fine," he said between clenched teeth.

John turned his attention back to his patient. "I want you to stay in bed for the rest of the afternoon. You've been traumatized. Your body needs to recover." He frowned. "I've been out in the sun too long," he said. "I forgot to ask your name."

The woman smiled. "You had a few other things on your mind. I'm..." She paused, her mouth open. Her lips moved, but no sound emerged. The smile faded and her eyes widened slightly. Fingers fluttered as her hand reached out into air, grasping for something he couldn't see.

She stared at John. "I don't know my name."

Chapter Two

Jarrett sat behind his desk and squeezed his Mont Blanc pen. He waited until his friend had poured himself a glass of Scotch from the decanter on the shelf on the far wall. When John had taken a swallow and crossed to the window he spoke.

"What's the prognosis?"

John shrugged. "I did as thorough an examination as I could. Good vital signs, no evidence of internal injuries. There are some bruises from her run-in with the cliff and she's not going to feel a hundred percent for a day or so, but aside from that, she's in great shape." He stared expectantly, as if waiting for Jarrett to comment on the double meaning in the last comment.

Jarrett ignored him. Yes, he'd noticed the mystery woman had a nice body. So what? Thousands, hundreds of thousands of women had nice bodies. That didn't mean he was interested in any of them.

"She needs rest," John continued when Jarrett was silent. "I'm sure you want her gone as quickly as possibly, but resist the urge to throw her out until tomorrow."

"I'm not completely inhuman," Jarrett said frostily.

"Nice to know. Sometimes I wonder."

Jarrett ignored that comment, too. "Is she faking?"

"The amnesia?" John shrugged. "It's hard to tell. Head injuries are tricky. We understand so little of the brain and how it heals. Often this kind of amnesia is bought on by a traumatic incident. It's usually temporary and disappears on its own. On the other hand—"

"Of course she's faking," Jarrett interrupted. "And she conveniently lost her identification or left it behind."

"That would be your professional opinion?"

"I know women." Jarrett stared out the window, forcing himself to see the blue sky and glittering water beyond. While he didn't appreciate the view as much as he should, at least he could focus on it instead of the past. Anything was better than remembering.

John took another swallow of Scotch, then sat in the chair in front of Jarrett's desk. "If you know she's faking, why bother with me?"

"I've been down this road before. I won't be played for a fool."

"Ah, I understand." John smoothed a hand over his thinning hair. "I wasn't aware you were being stalked by a series of women who had lost their memories. Under the circumstances, then, you would definitely have more insight into this problem than I do. I bow to your superior knowledge and experience."

Jarrett narrowed his gaze. "You're not the least bit amusing."

John grinned. "Hey, I think I'm funny and, in the end, isn't that what matters?"

Jarrett kept his expression cold.

John sighed. "All right. We'll do it your way, but I think you're taking this too much to heart. It *is* possible that the mystery lady is just that, a mystery. Not a stalker or a woman out to trick you into a relationship."

"I can't afford not to be careful." He stared at the man who, despite Jarrett's natural inclination to hold the world at bay, had become a friend. "You know some of what happened in my past, John, but you don't know everything that happened. I have to assume the worst. Especially now that Anna Jane is with me. Her safety is my responsibility."

"Do you want her to come stay with me tonight?" he asked.

Jarrett raised his eyebrows. "She's only nine, John. You can't leave her alone."

"I know that." John sounded hurt. "I'm a doctor. I wouldn't mind staying in for the evening. I could use the rest."

"With your schedule, I'm not surprised."

John's exploits were legendary. His beachfront home had played host to a legion of lovely ladies. Most were resort guests who stayed with him for the length of their vacation. Some were hotel staffers. He never claimed to want more than a passing affair, and the women seemed pleased to comply.

"Anna Jane will be safe enough here," Jarrett continued. "You said the woman can be moved in the morning."

"All she needs is a good night's sleep. Besides, you can use the time to figure out if she's faking or not," the doctor said. "If she is, as you said, playing you for a

fool, you should be able to trip her up. If she's the genuine article, then you've simply spent a few hours in the
company of a lovely lady. There are worse fates.''

Jarrett ignored John's last comment. He didn't share
his friend's desire for constant female companionship.
''If the amnesia is real, what will happen?''

''I'm not sure. Her memory could return in pieces or
it could all come back at once. She'll probably remember
odd bits of information while forgetting seemingly simple
things. The brain is a complex organ.'' John finished his
Scotch. ''In the meantime, what are you going to do with
her?''

''She's not my responsibility. In the morning Frank
will drive her back to the resort. My housekeeper's the-
ories aside, I doubt she came from one of the neighboring
islands. I'm sure she has a few friends who are expecting
her back tonight. I'll return her to them.''

John rose to his feet. ''It's your call. But I can't believe
you're not the least bit curious about her.''

''Why would I be?''

''A beautiful woman washes up on your private beach.
She doesn't know who she is or where she's from. Think
of the mystery, the fantasy, the possibilities.''

Jarrett grimaced. ''The lawsuit.''

''You have no romance in your soul.''

True. He didn't have a soul at all. At least, not one
he'd felt recently. He'd turned off all his emotions a long
time ago. Life was easier once he'd learned not to feel.
He depended on logic and action. They were enough.

John walked to the door. ''Call me if anything
changes, but she should be fine. Don't forget to feed her
dinner. You could even invite her to share the meal with
you.''

''Goodbye, John.''

John winked. "Lucky SOB. Why doesn't stuff like this happen to me?" He waved and left.

Jarrett stared after him. If John knew the truth, he wouldn't want Jarrett's life or his past.

Anna Jane paused outside her uncle's study. The big door stood open. She didn't want to go inside. She didn't want to tell her uncle the truth and have him be mad at her. Maybe she didn't have to. Maybe Leona wouldn't say anything and she could just—

Nana B. had taught her to be honest. Her nanny often explained that honesty wasn't just about telling the truth. It was also about living a life without deceit and manipulation, although Anna Jane still wasn't sure what manipulation was.

She swallowed hard once, then tapped softly on the open door. Her uncle looked up and saw her. For a moment, his hard expression softened as he beckoned her inside.

"I would have thought you would be with our mystery guest," he said lightly.

"She's sleeping. Dr. John says she's going to be all right. Is that true?"

Her uncle nodded. "She'll be fine. I'm sure she has friends waiting for her at the resort. As soon as they get in touch with the hotel manager, he'll tell them she's okay. They can come and get her in the morning."

Anna Jane reached into her shorts pocket and pulled out a damp piece of paper. After smoothing it flat, she passed it to her uncle.

"She *did* get my note. That's why she tried to find me. It's my fault she almost d-drowned."

Her uncle scanned the note, then turned it over and looked at the map. "You put this in a bottle?" he asked.

"Yes," she whispered.

He frowned. "The tide would have carried it north, not south," he said, almost to himself. "Where did you drop it in the water?"

"I know I'm not allowed down to the beach by myself. I didn't go there. I put the bottle in the pond by the house. The stream carried it away."

"That makes sense. That's an inland waterway. Your bottle never made it to the ocean. So our mystery guest could only have come from the resort." He gave her a smile. "Thanks for telling me. This will make her identity easier to discover."

"I didn't mean to hurt anyone."

"The woman isn't really hurt, Anna Jane. None of this is your fault," he said.

She nodded, hoping he would motion her closer and hug her. But he didn't. He seemed to be waiting to see if she had more to discuss.

"Can she come downstairs for dinner?" she asked.

The faint tightening of his features told her Uncle Jarrett wasn't pleased with her request, but he didn't refuse her. "If she feels up to it."

"Thank you," she whispered, and told herself she should leave. But there was something else she had to know. "Why don't you like her?"

His dark gaze captured hers. She bit down hard on her lower lip and braced herself for an explosion. But her uncle was silent as he studied her face. She wondered what he saw there. Nana B. used to say she looked a lot like her mother. Anna Jane knew that wasn't true. Her mother had been beautiful, like people on television.

"I don't dislike her," Uncle Jarrett said at last. "I don't know her. I'm a little concerned about her showing up the way she did. Now that I know she actually read your note..." His voice trailed off. "Don't worry, Anna Jane. Everything is going to be fine."

Perhaps, she thought. If anyone had the power to make something all right, it was her uncle. After all, he ran an empire.

She escaped the office and raced upstairs. She made it nearly to the top before feeling the hot breath of the creatures who lived below. With a burst of speed, she jumped to the second floor. She was safe on the landing. At least for now.

Maybe it was his work that made Uncle Jarrett angry all the time, she thought. Nana B. had explained that being a grown-up was difficult at times. Uncle Jarrett had lots of responsibility. And now he had her. She was a big responsibility. She'd heard her mother telling someone that once when she'd been on the phone.

"I don't mean to be," Anna Jane whispered as she made her way to her room.

She was halfway down the hall when she noticed that the guest-room door stood open. Her steps slowed. What was the woman like? How had she come to be washed up on the beach? Did she really not remember who she was?

Anna Jane crept to the open door and peered inside the room. The strange woman sat in front of the dresser, staring at herself in the mirror. She wore a thick white terry-cloth robe. Her hair was loose, and the soft-looking gold-blond strands tumbled over her shoulders.

Anna Jane fingered her own dark hair. She wondered what it was like to have hair the color of gold. Did it feel different?

"Are you spying or waiting for an invitation?" the woman asked.

Anna Jane jumped slightly, then entered the room. "Both," she admitted.

The woman turned to face her and smiled. "You're welcome to keep me company."

She had wide green eyes and a nice mouth. Anna Jane would bet that when the bruises were gone, the woman would be very pretty. Right now, though, it was hard to tell. She had a gash across the pale skin on her forehead. Bruises darkened the left side of her face.

"Who are you?" the woman asked.

"Anna Jane Quinlin."

"You live here on the island?" She frowned. "This is an island, isn't it?"

Anna Jane nodded. "My uncle owns it."

"Are you here on vacation?"

"No. My mother died and I had to come live here."

The woman's face softened with sympathy. "I'm so sorry. You must miss her."

"Yes. Of course," Anna Jane said automatically, tucking her right hand behind her back and crossing her fingers so the lie wouldn't count. It wasn't that she didn't miss her mother. She did. Sort of. The way she missed her favorite teacher or the housekeeper. But she didn't miss her mother the way this nice lady thought. She didn't cry for her at night. Those tears were reserved for Nana B. Anna Jane knew it was a sin to love Nana B. more than her own mother, but she couldn't change how she felt. She prayed for God to understand.

She tried to think of something to say to change the subject. Her gaze fell on the pile of clothes on the bed. "What are those?"

The woman sighed. "Your housekeeper brought them to me. I was only wearing a bathing suit and a pair of shorts, so I need something to wear. I'm just not sure what I like. Or what I used to like. It's very confusing."

Anna Jane walked over to the bed and fingered the top garment. There were shorts, T-shirts, sundresses, bathing suits, nightgowns. She picked up a white filmy nightie. "You wear this to bed," she said.

The woman smiled. "I remember that." She stood and approached the bed. A bright floral-print sundress lay to one side. "I was going to pick this one. What do you think?"

Anna Jane tilted her head to one side and studied her. "It's nice. You can wear your hair up on your head with some curls loose around your ears." She pointed to a big red-and-purple flower right in front. "That one matches your bruises."

She'd spoken without thinking, and instantly covered her mouth. "I'm sorry," she mumbled.

The woman laughed. "Don't be. You're exactly right." She cleared her throat. "Bruise wear," she said in a low voice, as if a commentator on television. "What all the models are sporting this summer in the tropics. Fall down and be fashionable."

Anna Jane giggled.

The woman plopped down on the bed and pulled Anna Jane down next to her. "You don't laugh enough," she said, putting her arm around her. "I can tell."

"Really?" Anna Jane asked, and leaned close. The embrace made her feel warm inside. "How can you know something like that?"

The woman's humor faded. "I don't know." She scrunched her eyes closed. "Isn't that strange. I can remember some things and I know you're not laughing very much these days, but I don't remember my own name."

"What's that like?"

"Scary," the woman said, looking at her. "I don't know who I am. I could be anyone."

"A princess?"

"Wouldn't that be nice. I'd like to be a princess with a beautiful castle."

"And a handsome prince."

The woman paused. "I'm not sure a handsome prince is always a good idea." She whispered in Anna Jane's ear. "Sometimes, when you're not looking, they can turn back into ugly toads."

Anna Jane laughed and the woman joined in.

"What's so funny?" a male voice asked.

Anna Jane looked up. "Uncle Jarrett! What are you doing up here?"

"I came to check on our guest." He turned to the woman and gave her a polite nod. "How do you feel?"

The woman's humor faded and her green eyes darkened. "Fine," she answered as she rose to her feet. She adjusted her terry-cloth robe, tightening the belt and tugging the V of the collar closer together.

Anna Jane slid off the bed. Uncle Jarrett was very angry. She could tell from the stiff set of his shoulders and the way his mouth straightened. It wasn't about her. That much she could figure out. Which left only the mystery lady. But why would she upset Uncle Jarrett?

"I don't think we've been properly introduced," he said, offering his hand. "I'm Jarrett Wilkenson."

"I know." The woman took the hand he held out and shook it quickly. "John, ah, Dr. Reed told me." She released him and clutched at the ends of the belt. "I appreciate your hospitality. I know I've inconvenienced you, but I promise I'll be on my way in the morning."

"On your way to where?"

She frowned. "Um, I'm not sure. John mentioned a hotel."

"The resort is about four miles from here."

"That's the one." The slender blonde smiled faintly. "At least if I had to lose my identity, I picked a beautiful place for it to happen."

"How convenient."

His voice said it wasn't convenient at all. The undercurrents in the room made Anna Jane uncomfortable. "Can you come downstairs for dinner?" she asked, blurting it out in an effort to distract them.

The woman looked startled. "That's so nice of you," she said. "I wouldn't want to intrude."

"You wouldn't. Uncle Jarrett's very busy. I usually eat alone."

"Oh." Their guest nodded. "I'd like that, then."

Jarrett had to admire her abilities. The woman's confusion was so real it was nearly tangible. If he hadn't already been suckered once by a woman, he might have bought into her act. The questions in her eyes, the faint trembling of her fingers, the way she kept tugging her robe belt tighter and tighter. All excellent devices designed to distract him from her true purpose.

She might be the best, but he was prepared. No one was going to get past his defenses again. If she thought she could use his niece to get to him, she was wrong.

"Dinner sounds like fun," he said, trying to keep his voice light. "I've been working too many hours lately. I think I'll join you."

"Really?" Anna Jane stared up at him, obviously thrilled.

He felt a pang of guilt and again questioned his sister's wisdom in naming him the guardian of her only child.

Anna Jane would have been better off with nearly anyone else. What did he know about raising a young girl?

He would have to learn, he told himself. His niece deserved the best he had to offer. Starting with his protection from unscrupulous females. At least he'd had the sense to come check on her. He'd lingered in the hallway before coming into the room. He'd heard the mystery woman's conversation with Anna Jane. The one in which the woman had said she wouldn't mind being a princess and living in a castle. He might not have a title, but he had plenty of land and money. More than enough to make certain kinds of women fantasize about happily ever after.

"Would you rather I stayed in my room?" the woman asked. Her expression bared her thoughts. She'd obviously figured out that he didn't want her alone with Anna Jane, but she wasn't sure why. Or she wanted him to think that.

"You're a guest in my house," Jarrett replied coolly. "Please make yourself at home." Which didn't really answer her question.

"I wish you knew your name," Anna Jane said. "We have to call you something."

Jarrett thought of several names, but none of them were suitable for a child's ears.

The woman shrugged. "Believe me, I wish I could remember, too."

"Maybe we can guess." The nine-year-old tilted her head. "You must have a pretty name. Like Heather or Julia. Sarina? Hannah?"

"None of those sounds right."

Anna Jane continued to try to come up with a name. Jarrett watched the two of them, watched the strange woman. Who was she? What did she hope to get from him—or Anna Jane? Despite the note, he doubted her motives were altruistic.

His gaze rose from her bare feet to her shapely calves, to her thighs, covered in part by the robe. Her upper body was concealed in the thick folds of terry cloth, but he remembered what she'd looked like on the beach, when she'd been wearing a bathing suit and shorts. As John had mentioned, she had a tempting figure. Her face was lovely, even with the bruises. She didn't look that old. Mid-twenties, maybe.

Something flickered low in his belly. For a second he thought it was recognition, then he realized it was something worse. Not to mention more dangerous.

Wanting. A whisper of heat blew across his dormant desire, causing slumbering need to stir restlessly. It was the last kind of trouble he needed in his life, and he firmly squashed the reaction. If he wanted a woman, he would return to the States and find an appropriate one. The kind of woman who understood that there was no potential for a long-term relationship.

Yet he wouldn't be leaving. Not only because he didn't want to abandon Anna Jane, but because he instinctively understood that the kind of woman he usually sought would not be able to help him this time.

"None of them sound right?" Anna Jane asked.

"I'm sorry. I wish I could think of my name." The woman rubbed her temples. "I can't believe this. It doesn't make sense."

Tell me about it, Jarrett thought grimly.

"Then we'll have to pick one," Anna Jane said. "Did you have a favorite?"

"You decide."

"Uncle Jarrett?"

"I'm staying out of it."

Anna Jane pursed her lips. "You were in the water, which is sort of like being a mermaid. What if we call you Ariel? She's the mermaid in the Disney movie."

"Ariel?" The woman repeated the name. "Fine, if you like it." She glanced at Jarrett. "Any objections?"

"No." He glanced at his watch. "I have to make a call to the West Coast. I'll see you two at dinner."

"Can I stay here with Ariel?" Anna Jane asked.

He looked into her dark eyes. She asked for so little. There was no way she could suspect their visitor of being anything other than what she claimed. He nodded, then walked into the hall and headed for the stairs.

Ariel. It was just a name, he told himself, yet it suited the woman. He didn't want to think about that, nor did he want to think about how quickly Anna Jane had taken to her. The last thing the child needed was to be hurt again. She'd been through enough.

He thought about returning to "Ariel's" room and warning her off. But he didn't. Mostly because she seemed to talk to the girl so easily. It was a skill he'd yet to master. Whenever he was around his niece, he didn't know what to say to her. He sensed she needed something from him, but what?

I usually eat alone. Anna Jane's words came back to him. He hadn't meant that to happen, for the child to be so solitary. His hotels were all around the world and the various time differences meant he was on the phone at odd hours. Had he really left her to eat on her own so many times?

He thought about the past few days and realized he had. Too many conference calls and too much work. He'd neglected Anna Jane. He resolved to make sure that didn't happen again. The first thing he had to do was get their mysterious guest out of his life. Then he would concentrate on his niece.

Chapter Three

Not knowing how else to wear her hair, Ariel had taken Anna Jane's suggestion that she pile it on top of her head. She'd handled the gold-blond curls easily, quickly scooping them into order and securing the style with pins from a makeup kit Leona had lent her.

Now Ariel stared into the vanity mirror at her dresser, studying the results. Feathered bangs covered her forehead but did nothing to conceal the bruises and scrapes along the left side of her face and the gash above her eyebrow. She touched the swollen area, wincing slightly at the pain. With her fingers she traced the shape of her nose, then her mouth, finally cupping her undamaged cheek.

No doubt like many women she spent a small portion of each day staring into a mirror. Perhaps just to make sure her skin was clean, or maybe to apply makeup. As a teenager she would have examined her features, trying to decide if she was pretty or not. A person would grow familiar with lines and planes, tiny imperfections, freckles, curves, coloring. Yet the face staring back at her was a stranger's. She would have sworn, under oath, with her hand on a Bible, that she'd never seen it before in her life.

And yet that face was hers.

Ariel sucked in a breath as the room tilted slightly. She sensed that the dizziness came from disbelief rather than from a physical reaction. She felt disconnected from her surroundings, and there were some aches from her close encounter with that cliff, but otherwise her body felt fine. It was her head that had her worried.

She stood and walked to the door. Dinner would be served in a few minutes, and she didn't want to keep her host waiting. She didn't have to be a rocket scientist to figure out Jarrett Wilkenson was the kind of man who expected things to happen on his timetable and not anyone else's.

As she reached for the door handle, a voice whispered at the back of her mind. It told her to turn around and take one last look in the mirror—just to make sure she looked all right. Something about the voice, something familiar, told her she'd heard it all her life. That she made a habit of checking in the mirror one last time. Just to make sure her slip wasn't showing or that she'd hadn't accidentally worn the wrong shoes. Most likely she'd always heeded the voice and checked her appearance. But not this time. Ariel knew what she would find when she looked in the mirror. She knew she would stare into a stranger's eyes, and she couldn't face that right now.

She stepped into the hallway. The doctor had cautioned her that trying to force memories wasn't going to work. With her kind of trauma, what was needed was time and rest. Until she had a life to return to, time wasn't going to be a problem. She had plenty. Resting, on the other hand, might be more of an issue. How was she supposed to relax when she didn't know who she was?

This kind of thing doesn't happen to normal people, Ariel told herself. Instantly the questions formed. How did she know normal people didn't lose their memories? How did she know *she* was normal? Did she usually make it a habit to talk to herself?

"No memory *and* crazy," she murmured as she started down the stairs. "There's a combination you don't see often enough."

She was still smiling when Anna Jane called to her.

"Ariel! You look so pretty. That dress is nice." The young girl stood in the foyer. "Leona says there's fresh fish for dinner. Fish is icky, but she makes it taste good. There's salad and cake for dessert."

Ariel's stomach growled and she touched it. "Gee, I wasn't hungry until you started talking about food, but now I'm starving." She made her way down the stairs. "I'm glad Dr. Reed said it was all right for me to come downstairs."

"Me, too." Anna Jane seemed to focus on the stairs.

Ariel turned and looked at them. "What's wrong?"

The little girl shrugged. "Nothing. It's just—" She wore a dark peach T-shirt and matching shorts that accentuated her tan. They'd been the same clothes Ariel had seen her in when she'd first awakened, and there wasn't a smudge on them. Anna Jane was too young to be keeping her clothes that clean. She must not be playing enough.

Ariel shook her head. How on earth could she make that kind of judgment? How could she know that?

Anna Jane took a step toward her and lowered her

voice. "Sometimes, when I go up the stairs alone, I worry about monsters waiting to snap at my heels." She paused, obviously waiting to be told she was imagining things.

Ariel crouched down so they were at eye level. "This is a big house," she said. "I would guess there are lots of places for monsters to hide. If I see them, I'll point them out to your uncle and he'll get rid of them. In the meantime, if I'm around, I'm happy to come up the stairs with you."

Anna Jane gave her a wide smile. "Thank you. I knew you'd understand."

Ariel wondered how the girl could be so certain. Nothing felt real. Maybe that's what was going on. Maybe she was just dreaming about everything. That would explain her knowledge of child psychology. Of course, one would think that if this was her dream, she would remember her own name.

The girl's smile faded. "Are you mad at me?"

"What?" Ariel asked, baffled.

"For sending the note in the bottle. That's what brought you here." Anna Jane clasped her hands together and twisted her fingers. "I said that I wanted a friend. I didn't mean for you to get hurt."

Ariel touched her shoulder. "Honey, that's not your fault. It's no one's fault. Dr. Reed told me about the note, and explained about the high tide in the cove. There's no way you could have known I would come that way. It's fine. Really."

"Promise?" Anna Jane asked.

"Swear." Ariel made a cross over her left breast. "I wasn't really hurt. Just a few scratches. They'll heal. I'm sure I had a bag or purse that got washed away, but that kind of stuff is replaceable. Don't worry."

"But you don't remember your name."

She did have a point. "I will. In time." At least, that's what the good doctor promised. Please, God, let him be right.

"Do you like the one I picked for you?"

"Ariel is a pretty name. Thank you." In fact, it was surprisingly easy to claim it as her own. Probably because she had nothing to compare it to. It wasn't as if she were having to remember new lines and forget old ones. Parts of her memory were so blank, she was grateful to fill them with anything.

"I wonder if I'll forget everything that's happening while I can't remember," she said more to herself.

"Huh?" Anna Jane frowned, drawing her delicate eyebrows together.

"When I get my memory back, will I remember what I'm doing now? While I can't remember who I am?"

"Oh. I don't know."

"Me, either."

"We'll have to ask Dr. Reed when next he visits." The male voice came from nowhere.

Ariel spun toward the sound and found Jarrett standing halfway down the stairs. She hadn't noticed him at all. He'd appeared as if by magic. Just as he had earlier in her bedroom.

"You move very quietly," she said, trying to shake off the feeling of being caught doing something she shouldn't.

"You were engrossed in your conversation. I didn't want to interrupt."

Oh, sure. She believed that. Despite the instinctive urge to flee or hide behind Anna Jane, Ariel forced herself to stand her ground and hold his gaze.

He was, she admitted grudgingly, the most handsome man she'd ever seen. Of course, the only men she could remember were Frank, the middle-aged gardener, and John Reed, the physician. But that didn't matter. Ariel knew in her gut that she could stare at a thousand men and none of them would come close to Jarrett Wilkenson.

He stood a couple of inches over six feet, with dark hair that had grown past conservative to flirt with the collar of his open-neck shirt. Dark eyes seemed to steal the light from the room without reflecting any in return. No doubt the man had the physical ability to smile, but he had yet to use it in her presence and she wasn't holding her breath until he did. Broad shoulders tapered into a trim waist, while his khaki trousers hinted at the strength of his thighs below.

He was a dangerous man. She didn't need memories to figure that out.

"Shall we go in to dinner?" he asked as he continued down the stairs. "I can smell Leona's cooking from here."

She waited politely until he'd reached the foyer, then allowed him to motion her toward the dining room.

Anna Jane chatted on as if the undercurrents between the adults didn't affect her. When they reached the set table, Ariel was surprised when Jarrett took the time to hold out a chair for her. She half expected him to pull it back and let her fall. Instead, he made sure she was comfortable before going to his own seat at the head.

Ariel glanced around at the room. The table could easily seat eight, and judging from the chairs pressed up against the wall, there were several extensions to handle a large dinner party. Wide windows allowed her to see out to the garden and the private beach beyond. On the wall to her left stood a huge china cabinet. To her right was a wooden buffet that looked antique.

"I heard you and Anna Jane discussing the note she

wrote," Jarrett said, pulling white wine from a waiting ice bucket and removing the cork. "Do you remember it?"

Ariel thought for a second. "Not a word."

"Perhaps seeing it would help." He set the cork on the table in front of Anna Jane. The young girl picked it up and sniffed. She nodded regally.

"A nice year, a little fruity," she intoned. "I think it will do for the likes of you, but I prefer something more dairy." She picked up her glass of milk and took a swallow.

"Thank you, madam," Jarrett said, and gave the girl a wink.

Ariel clutched the side of the table to keep from sliding off her chair in shock. Was that a sense of humor she'd just seen? From Jarrett Wilkenson? Maybe he wasn't as stiff as she'd first thought.

Then he turned his frosty gaze on her and she knew all bets were off. She hadn't imagined it. He *didn't* like her. Because she'd invaded his home, or maybe for reasons she would never know. It didn't matter. She only had to get through the dinner. In the morning she would go to the hotel and start figuring out a way to reconnect with her life.

"I have the note with me," he said when he finished pouring them each a glass of wine. He removed the paper from his pants pocket and placed it on the table in front of her. "You do remember how to read, don't you?"

"Of course," she said without thinking as she picked up the note. She made the mistake of glancing at him and saw something hard and cold flash in his eyes. Satisfaction and what else? Why did he care if she could read or not? Unless he didn't believe her.

She didn't want to consider that, so she turned her

attention to the piece of paper in her hand. She read the message three times, then turned it over and studied the map.

"I've never seen this before," she told Jarrett as she returned the sheet to him.

"As you know, you had it in your shorts pocket when you washed ashore."

She didn't know how that could be. How could she have just lost pieces of her life? Frustration filled her. Frustration and a touch of fear. "This is crazy," she said. "Is there someone I can talk to? Maybe the local police have a missing persons report or something."

"There are no police. St. Alicia is a private island and mostly uninhabited. Except for the resort guests and staff, there are no other residents. When necessary, I am the law here."

Great. He probably made one interesting dictator. She would have to remember not to commit a crime while under his jurisdiction.

"Don't worry, Ariel. I've spoken to my hotel manager. He's having the staff check reservations and talk with the guests. I'm sure by the time we've finished Leona's dinner, your family will have been found. Perhaps when you're with them, your memory will return."

Before she could comment, Leona began serving the meal. As promised, the food was excellent. Jarrett was the perfect host, keeping conversation flowing and topics innocuous. But every now and then Ariel caught a glimpse of something in his eyes. Or she heard a thread of rage in his voice. He was furious with her, and she still didn't have a clue as to what she'd done wrong. One thing was certain—she had to get out of here, and fast.

Let there be a family, she prayed quietly as dessert

was brought to the table. Maybe a couple of burly brothers to threaten Jarrett.

"Where were you born?" Anna Jane asked, then covered her mouth with her hand. "Oops. I forgot."

"No, don't apologize," Ariel said. "I think it's probably good to ask me questions. I can't figure out what I know and don't know until we talk about it." She glanced at Jarrett. "That is, if you don't mind."

"Please," he said too graciously. "Discuss what you would like."

Sure. Let's talk about why you don't like me, she thought. "I don't know where I was born," she said instead. "But I think I'm American. Do I have an accent?"

"Not a regional one," Jarrett told her. "Not Southern or Eastern. I don't think you're from the Midwest. Maybe somewhere west?"

"There's lots of states out west," Anna Jane said. "Arizona, Nevada, Washington, California and Oregon. Oh, Utah and Idaho, too."

Ariel shook her head and forced herself to smile. "At least we know you've learned your geography."

"I like that subject," the nine-year-old said. "I like looking at maps and stuff." Her chin dropped slightly. "I hope they study that at my new school."

"New school?" Ariel repeated.

Anna Jane nodded. "I haven't gone since I've been here, but I have to start after Christmas, right, Uncle Jarrett?"

"We'll figure something out," he told her.

He must have seen Ariel's confusion. "My sister passed away a few weeks ago," he added. "Anna Jane has been with me since then."

Ariel's heart ached for the little girl. The loss of a parent was horrible. She might not know why she understood the pain, but she did. Impulsively, she reached across the table and took the child's hand in hers.

"I'm sorry," she said, and squeezed her fingers.

Anna Jane smiled gratefully. "I'm glad you're here, Ariel. I'm glad I sent that note and you were the one to find it."

Ariel nodded as if she, too, were glad. But she wasn't. If she hadn't found the note and nearly drowned in the cove, she wouldn't have lost her memory. Right now she would be back in her own life. Whatever and wherever that was.

Jarrett listened a couple more minutes, then thanked his hotel manager for the information. "I'll talk to you in the morning," he promised, and hung up.

From where he was sitting, he could see his guest pacing in the hallway outside his office. She moved with an easy grace that brought to mind unwelcome images of long, slender legs and gold-blond hair tumbling free. He pushed the thoughts away, just as he pushed away the ridiculous notion that he was reluctant to tell her what he'd found out because he didn't want to disappoint her.

As if sensing his attention, Ariel turned toward him, her expression questioning. He motioned her forward. As her hips swayed sensuously and the movement tempted him, he reminded himself he wasn't sure what her game was. Had she come to the island with a purpose and had finding the note been a lucky break, or had finding the note made her act impulsively? He told himself it didn't matter. Either way, she was out for what she could get. No way in hell would he let her take advantage of him...or Anna Jane.

But as she paused in front of his desk and shifted her weight nervously, he had to admit she was good. About the best he'd ever seen. From the confusion darkening her eyes to the color of jade, right down to the faint tremor in her hands, she was convincing in her performance. She belonged on the stage.

"I've spoken with the hotel manager," he said, motioning to the chair in front of her.

She sank into it and stared at him. The corners of her mouth quivered. "I assume the news isn't good."

"There isn't any news. So far no one has reported a missing guest. Nor is there a single reservation. My staff has checked back as far as two weeks. This time of year we generally get couples and families. Most of the employees with direct guest contact have been questioned, but no one remembers a woman of your description."

Ariel looked as shocked as if he'd hit her. The color drained from her face and she clutched the chair arms. "No one is looking for me?" she asked quietly. "No one at all?"

The pang of emotion was so unfamiliar, it took him a moment to identify it. Compassion. For her? He didn't like that.

"It's possible there hasn't been enough time. You only disappeared this morning. Perhaps they haven't noticed."

She glanced at the beautiful antique grandfather clock in the corner of his office. "It's nearly nine. Someone somewhere has to know I'm missing. I have to have family."

"Why?"

"I—" She clamped her lips together. Her expression tightened as she obviously fought back tears. She stiffened, then leaned against the back of the chair. "There has to be someone in my life. I refuse to believe I'm completely alone."

"Many people are alone. Until you regain your memory..." He paused. Keeping the sarcasm out of his voice took a little effort. "Until that time, it's pointless to assume anything about yourself."

"I would hate to think no one would miss me," she said, more to herself than him.

He thought about asking why. Being alone was hardly a curse. He'd spent much of his life that way. These days it was by choice. When alive, his sister had pressured him to visit, but more often than not, he'd refused. Being on his own was always easier than being with other people. He supposed that if something had happened to him, his sister would have missed him. But not overly much. Compared to how she'd mourned the loss of her beloved husband, he doubted missing a brother would have set her back much. While he often thought of his sister, her loss hardly affected his day-to-day life. Except for the arrival of his niece. Perhaps it wasn't the way the rest of the world chose to live, but he was very content.

Ariel shrugged. "I suppose there's nothing I can do tonight. In the morning, well, I'll figure out something."

At that moment she looked as lost and alone as Anna Jane had when she'd first arrived. Despite his cynicism, Jarrett found himself wanting to offer words of comfort. He had to hold back an invitation that she stay in the house until she recovered her memory.

She hadn't lost her memory in the first place, he reminded himself. Perhaps it was time for both of them to admit that truth.

He leaned back in his chair and met her gaze. "It's not going to work," he began conversationally.

"What are you talking about?"

"This act of yours. It's very good. I've nearly been taken in, which is impressive, because I don't impress easily."

She blinked twice. "What are you talking about?"

"Women have shown up in my boardroom, my bedroom and even my shower. I've received proposals and propositions by letter, E-mail and fax. While the amnesia routine is unique, and you get points for risking your life in the cove, it's still not going to work. You're not going to get your hands on me or my fortune. Don't bother even thinking about using my niece to get to me, either."

The rest of the color drained from Ariel's face. Her lips parted, but she couldn't seem to speak. Jarrett, who considered himself a quick study and a great judge of character, allowed himself a moment of doubt.

"Is that what you think this is about?" she asked, her voice shaking with emotion. "You think I'm faking this so I can be with you?" She emphasized the last word using a tone usually reserved to describe cockroaches and roadkill.

"To be honest," he said, "yes."

"I see. What an interesting world you live in, Jarrett Wilkenson. Until this moment I had envied you your beautiful house and your beautiful island, but you've cured me of that. If fear and distrust are the price you pay, I'm not the least bit interested. As for wanting you—" she rose to her feet and placed her hands flat on the desk as she bent toward him "—you're good-looking, but not *that* good-looking. I might not remember who I am or where I'm from, but I'm willing to bet I'm not nearly desperate enough to risk anything to be with a man like you." She turned and started for the door.

He respected backbone. "If you mean what you say, then you won't object to being driven back to the hotel in the morning."

She spun toward him. "I'd prefer to be driven back tonight."

"Dr. Reed insisted that you stay put for tonight. He's concerned about your head injury."

Wounded pride radiated from her like heat from a fire. He could practically see it. "I suppose you want to blame me for that, too."

"No. John made the recommendation without any help from anyone. But it is convenient...for you."

"Are you always this much of a bastard?"

"When I have to be. My driver will be ready at nine tomorrow morning. See that you are, too. I'm sure by then whomever you're traveling with will have claimed you. If not, a single room will be found. You will, of course, be a guest of the hotel until your identity can be restored."

"I don't want your free room. Someone will be waiting for me."

She said the words with conviction, but they both knew she might be wrong. Jarrett had expected a traveling companion of either gender to be kicking up a fuss at the mystery woman's absence. He didn't like the fact that no one had. If she wasn't with people and the hotel had no single reservations, then who was she?

She continued to stare at him, as if she wanted to say more. Then her shoulders slumped slightly. For a moment, silhouetted by the door frame, she again looked lost and alone.

Deliberately, refusing to acknowledge her or speak to her again, he turned his attention to some papers on his desk. He read the balance sheet three times before it made sense, then wrote a couple of notes in the margin. When he finally looked up, she was gone.

Jarrett tapped on his niece's half-open bedroom door. "Come in," she called.

He entered and found Anna Jane sitting up in bed, reading. He glanced at his watch. "Don't you have a bedtime?"

She smiled. "Yes, and it's nearly an hour past it. Are you here to tell me to turn out the light?"

"I'm here to tuck you in."

"Really?"

Her smile widened with pleasure, and Jarrett's guilt returned. It was a simple task. One he'd promised himself he would perform faithfully. But time had a way of speeding past. Three times in the past week he'd looked up and found it was already near midnight. He'd come to the girl's room, but she had been asleep.

As she lay back on the bed, he took the book from her and looked at the spine. The story was about a boy and his horse. Jarrett remembered the tale from his own childhood.

"I read this one," he said. "It's good."

"I've read it, too. I liked the series so much I'm reading it again."

As he smoothed the covers over her, he noticed the neat stack of boxes in the corner. Unopened board games commingled with puzzles, dolls and an elaborate kit to make plastic jewelry.

"You don't like your toys?" he asked.

Her brown eyes, so much like his sister's, glanced away. "They're very nice. Thank you for getting them for me."

"But?"

She sighed. "It's not fun playing with all that stuff by myself."

He sat on the edge of the bed and took her hand in his. Her fingers were small, the nails clean and neatly trimmed. What kind of life was this for her? he wondered.

"I'm sorry, Anna Jane. I should have thought of that."

"You're very busy. I'm an unexpected responsibility."

She said the words easily, as if she'd heard them many times before. Who had been saying them to her? Not him. Her mother? The nanny she'd had after Nana B. had retired?

"You're not a responsibility, you're my niece. I should have picked out better toys."

"They would be fun with someone to play with. Maybe Ariel could stay and take care of me until she remembers who she is."

He was careful to keep his hold on her hand relaxed, even though every muscle in his body tightened in protest. Why hadn't he seen this coming? He'd heard the easy conversation between them, had seen the way Ariel had comforted her when they'd talked of her mother's death. It made perfect sense.

"Ariel has her own life," he said. "There are people who miss her."

"What if there aren't? No one has found her family yet, have they?"

"No, but—"

"Why can't she stay here until they do? I'll keep her out of the way, Uncle Jarrett. You won't even know she's here."

Despite his irritation at the thought, he had to smile. He touched Anna Jane's soft cheek. "That's logic you use to keep a puppy, not a grown woman."

She wrinkled her nose. "I still thought it might work. Please?"

Ariel stay here? Could he stand it? He wanted her gone. If not for John's request that she not be moved, he would have had her taken back to the hotel after dinner. While a part of him was willing to admit there was a tiny possibility she might not be faking her amnesia, the rest of him didn't care. Either way, she was trouble.

"I'll think about it," he said at last.

Anna Jane sighed. "What kind of 'I'll think about it' do you mean?"

"What?"

"When Mama said she would think about it, she meant no. Nana B. meant she really would think about it. Which one do you mean?"

Jarrett bent and kissed her forehead. "I mean I'll consider your request. But if Ariel stays, you have to feed her and take her for walks every day. And make sure she doesn't chew on my shoes."

Anna Jane giggled. As she wrapped her arms around his neck and hugged him tight, he wondered what he'd done to deserve her affection.

Chapter Four

Ariel looked out the window at the bright morning light. She was sick of staring into the mirror and trying to find something familiar. She'd spent more than an hour last night looking at her face from different angles, trying to catch a glimpse of something that might spark a memory. Instead all she'd generated was a massive headache and a feeling of desolation that had yet to go away.

Amnesia played well in the movies, but in real life it was very frightening to have one's past disappear.

She glanced at the clock and frowned. It was nearly eight-thirty. In another half hour she would go downstairs and be returned to the hotel. If that's where she'd come from. Her discomfort wasn't from the thought of leaving. Jarrett had made it quite clear she wasn't welcome here and, under the circumstances, she was pleased to be leaving. What upset her was there was still no news. She'd been so sure she would wake up to remember who she was. Barring that, she'd been certain Leona would deliver good news with breakfast. Parents who were distraught over her absence. A sibling or two who'd been frantic all night. A worried boyfriend.

She grimaced at the last thought, somehow knowing no boyfriend or husband had a place in her life right now. But she wouldn't mind a sister or two.

Ariel turned to the bed. Leona had insisted she keep the resort wear she'd brought the previous afternoon. Ariel hadn't asked about it, assuming Jarrett kept a supply on hand for whatever company he might have visiting him. Although, judging from their conversation last night, he really wasn't the type to do much entertaining.

She bent and fingered the sundress she'd worn to dinner. It was pretty but seemed a little dressy for daytime. She pushed it aside in favor of shorts and a T-shirt in bright rose.

Clothing decided, she turned reluctantly to the mirror and stared at her hair. It lay in loose waves over her shoulders. The layered style suggested she'd had it trimmed recently. Familiar actions tugged at the edges of her memory, as if she was supposed to do something with her hair. But what?

She pulled out the small chair in front of the vanity and sank down. What was the routine she performed every morning without thinking? How did her hands move, her fingers twist and bend and secure while she planned the day ahead?

Trying not to focus too much, she reached for a hairbrush and closed her eyes. Maybe if she cleared her mind, her body would take over. She allowed herself to relax as she thought about what she would like to eat for breakfast. Maybe cereal with fruit, or some toast.

But the brush didn't feel familiar in her hand and she

got caught up in trying to remember what she usually ate in the morning. She tossed the brush down and reached behind to pull her hair into a ponytail.

Instead her fingers began pulling sections of hair apart, then weaving them in a swift series of complex moves. Ariel held her breath as she quickly finished a perfect French braid. She wasn't sure which excited her more. The fact that she could do the braid or that she knew what it was called.

She stood and turned so she could admire her handiwork from the rear. There was a knock on her closed bedroom door. "Come in," she called.

The door opened and Jarrett stepped inside. Ariel belatedly realized she was dressed in only a towel and lunged for her borrowed robe lying across the foot of the bed. She wrapped it around herself hastily and tightened the belt.

"You could have announced yourself," she said, fighting embarrassment.

"I knocked."

"I know, but I thought it was Anna Jane or Leona."

"Perhaps you should have asked instead of assuming."

"Thank you. I'll remember that."

He filled her doorway. Perhaps in deference to the fact that he worked on a tropical island, Jarrett didn't wear a suit or tie. Instead he wore a red polo shirt tucked into worn jeans. She could see the muscle definition of his arms and chest under the smooth material.

She jerked her mind away from his masculine presence and reminded herself this wasn't a social call. Last night Jarrett had made his opinion of her very clear. His words still stung.

"Come in," she said, motioning to the chair in front of the vanity. "I'll just be a second."

She scooped up the shorts and T-shirt she'd picked out earlier and headed for the bathroom.

As she dressed quickly she consoled herself with the thought that she'd found another piece of her personality. She'd been embarrassed that Jarrett had caught her wearing a towel, so she was modest and definitely not promiscuous. Thank goodness. She wished she could share her observation, but Jarrett didn't strike her as the kind of person who had much of a sense of humor.

The thought made her smile, and her lips were still curved up when she opened the bathroom door. Jarrett's neutral expression squashed her amusement like an empty peanut shell. She squared her shoulders and glanced at the clock radio on the nightstand.

"If you're here to make sure I'm downstairs in time to meet your driver, you don't have to worry. I have no intention of being late."

"Not at all," he said, and nodded at the bed. "Please sit down."

She perched on the edge of the mattress and placed her hands in her lap. If he wanted to play at being socially correct, she could do the same.

When she was settled, he drew in a breath. "I've spoken to my manager at the hotel. Despite the fact that we were all hoping family members would come forward to report you missing, no one has."

He continued talking, but Ariel didn't hear him. She couldn't. She focused on that single sentence, those cold words that cut her adrift from her hopes and left her floundering for support.

"No one?" she asked, interrupting him. "No one has reported me missing?"

"No."

It wasn't possible. It couldn't be. How could she be all alone in the world? It wasn't right. "No one wants me," she whispered, more to herself than him.

Jarrett cleared his throat. "I'm sure you have family. Just not here, at the resort."

She wanted to ask how he was sure. He couldn't be. He was just trying to say the right thing. Not to be kind, but so she wouldn't get hysterical or cause him any more trouble. If he even believed her at all. Along with this latest batch of bad news, she was still reeling from his assumption she was faking her condition in order to get close to him. Why would any woman try such a desperate tactic on a man like him?

She couldn't think about that now, she told herself. What was important was finding her life. "My room," she said as she received a burst of inspiration. "I haven't been in my room. The housekeeping staff only has to look for a room that hasn't been slept in."

"I wish it was that simple." He leaned back on the small chair and rested one ankle on the opposite knee. "Because of the location of St. Alicia, not to mention the limited amenities, many of our guests make trips to other islands. An unused bed isn't that unusual around here."

"What about the other—"

He held up a hand to stop her. "I've already sent word to the other islands," he said. "News about you will travel quickly. If you have family or friends on the other islands, they'll be able to get in touch with you here. It shouldn't take long. Not many women travel alone this time of year. Someone will report you missing."

The thought of other islands gave her a little hope, but in her gut she felt she'd only been on St. Alicia. Some shadow of the past flirted with her consciousness enough to make her certain of that. The same shadow offered comfort in the form of almost memories of someone, somewhere, caring about her. Despite the fact that no one was looking for her, she wasn't convinced she was completely alone. Then the rest of what he'd said sank in.

"What do you mean by 'this time of year'?"

"Christmas is in less than two weeks," he said.

She felt her mouth drop open, and she closed it. "You're kidding."

"No."

Christmas? Without family? It was too horrible to consider. "I had no idea."

"If you've lost your memory, that makes sense."

She wasn't sure if he was simply making conversation or getting in a dig, and she decided not to try to figure it out. "I sure couldn't tell from your house."

He frowned, dark eyebrows pulling together. "What do you mean?"

She shrugged. "Judging from the lack of decorations, it could be mid-April. What about wreaths and a tree? Maybe even some presents?"

"I don't bother with that kind of thing."

How sad, she thought. Even though he thought the worst of her and had flat-out told her so to her face, she couldn't escape the wave of compassion that swept through her. How could someone not bother with the holidays? They were a time for sharing. But Jarrett was the kind of man who probably shared as easily as he trusted.

She looked at him. That handsome face and tempting masculine body all wrapped around a cynical heart and a soul of ice. The beautiful package was a waste.

"It's not just you anymore," she said. "You have Anna Jane to think about. Jarrett, she needs this Christmas. Despite her mother's death, or maybe because of it, she has to know that her world is still going to go on. Being without her mother is going to make this Christmas awful for her, and you have to be prepared for that. She needs you to be there for her.''

His gaze narrowed. ''What makes you an expert?''

She paused. ''I'm not sure, but I know what I'm talking about.'' Did he think she was making this up, too? ''No matter what you think of me, please don't discount what I've said. I don't mean to be rude or anything, although based on what you said to me last night, I suppose I have the right, but you don't know your niece very well. She hasn't been here that long and she needs you to spend time with her. Only a very lonely child would go to all the trouble to send a note in a bottle.''

''I don't dispute the fact that this has been difficult for Anna Jane.''

And for you, too, she thought suddenly. Losing his sister and inheriting a child would have upset even someone as contained and controlled as this man.

''How well do you know her?'' she asked.

''I've met her a few times.''

''But no regular contact?''

''No.''

Ariel sighed. ''That's tough for both of you.'' She scooted forward, leaning toward him. ''Jarrett, she's just a scared little girl. Right now she needs stability and love more than anything.''

''Again, I ask what makes you an expert?''

''I don't know. But I'm as sure of this as I am—'' She stopped in midsentence. ''Well, I'm just sure.''

He didn't want to believe her. She could see the battle being waged inside him. He didn't like or trust her, yet he recognized the truth of her words and couldn't bring himself to discount her. At least she had to give him credit for caring about his niece.

Who was he, this dark, mysterious man who didn't know how to talk to a little girl? What events had made him so aloof and forced him to live in this place so far from the mainstream of life? Why was she foolish enough to be attracted to someone who wanted nothing to do with her?

"I'm going to assume from the conversation we had last night that you're not married," she said.

A raised eyebrow was his only response.

"I'll take that as a no. Too bad. A wife would have made things easier for Anna Jane."

"What about you?" he asked. "Any husbands lurking in the background?"

"No." Certainty made her speak without thinking. She rose to her feet. "No. I'm not married."

"What makes you so sure?"

She paced to the window, then turned back to him. "I know I'm not married. I mean, I *know* it. This is information about my life. Ask me another question. About anything."

"Any foreign languages?"

A part of her was surprised he was willing to play along. A part of her responded with the correct information. "Spanish, but not well."

"Did you go to college?"

"Yes."

"Where?"

She searched her mind. "I don't know."

"Are you an only child?"

"No."

"Brothers and sisters?"

Again, the frustrating grayness of a memory that

wouldn't cooperate. "Maybe. Yes." She shook her head. "I don't know."

"Are your parents alive?"

A sharp pain cut through her chest. She caught her breath. What did that mean? Pain at their passing, or pain for a separation caused by misunderstandings? "I don't know."

He tried a couple more questions before she stopped him.

"It's gone," she said. "Whatever I was in touch with is gone." She faced the window and clutched the sill. "I just want myself back. Why is that so difficult?"

Jarrett didn't answer. Actually, Ariel hadn't expected him to. After all, he thought this was all some kind of performance on her part. Frustration filled her.

"I'm not kidding," she went on, focusing on the incredible view of beach and sapphire blue ocean. "I know you don't believe me, but it's true. It's horrible, this feeling of being out in space without an anchor. I could be anyone. It's terrifying. What if I don't like who I am?" She laughed without humor. "Don't answer that one. I already know your opinion of me."

He didn't say anything and she thought he might have left the room. Then the skin on the back of her neck prickled and she knew he was still there, still watching her. No doubt thinking that she deserved an award for her acting ability. Damn the man.

"I'd better go downstairs and wait for your driver," she said, moving to the dresser where she'd left her shorts and bathing suit. They were the only clothes she'd been wearing the previous day. Anything else she'd had with her had been washed out to sea.

"What are you going to do at the hotel?"

She looked at him, trying to read something into the

question. "Are you reminding me I have no identification and no credit cards?"

"Of course not. A room will be provided for you until you figure things out. I meant what will you do with your time?"

"I don't know." She hadn't thought that far in advance. "Walk around and talk to guests, I suppose. Don't worry, I won't make trouble or be intrusive."

"I never thought you would be."

"Yeah, right. Does it matter what I do? I'll be out of your life, and that's the most important part."

"You're right about Anna Jane," he said. "I know she's a lonely child. I'm not sure what to do about it."

"Children aren't that complicated. Spend some time with her. Love her. It's a pretty simple formula."

"Business keeps me busy."

"As it's Christmas, I'll quote Charles Dickens's *A Christmas Carol*. 'Mankind is our business.' You might want to remember that, just in case you're due to be visited by three ghosts."

Jarrett Wilkenson actually smiled. The corners of his lips turned up and he flashed white teeth. Ariel staggered a step before she reclaimed her balance.

"Are you comparing me to Scrooge?" he asked.

"Yes."

She headed for the door.

"Ariel, I'd like to ask you something."

Oh, but she would have liked to have kept on walking. Turning her back on him and ignoring what he had to say would have given her great satisfaction. Manners made her pause. Not only was he her host, but he was going to be putting her up in his hotel for the next however long it took until she came up with a plan on her own.

She paused and leaned against the door frame.

"You responded to my niece's note. She thinks you were sent here for her."

"Yes, and you think this is all an elaborate trick. So either I had something planned in advance and got lucky with the note, or I found the note and made an impulsive decision to try and snare you. We've discussed this already. What's your point?"

It was much easier to speak her mind when she had her back to the man. If they were ever caught up in another argument, she would have to remember this strategy.

"Until you recover your memory, or someone comes looking for you, perhaps you would be more comfortable staying here. At the house. Being alone in a hotel can be very lonely. Especially during the holidays."

She clutched her clothes tightly to her chest and turned to face him. He had to be kidding. "You hate me."

"I don't know you well enough to hate you."

"Fine. You don't trust me and you doubt my story."

"True enough."

"Yet you'd invite me to move in to your home?"

"For the sake of my niece, who asked if you could stay, yes."

His dark eyes gave nothing away. Neither did his face. The man was good. She wouldn't want to play poker with him. Unless it was strip poker and in her best interest to lose.

Not sure where that thought had come from, she pushed it away. "This is crazy."

"It's your decision."

She thought about what he'd said. About the holidays being lonely in a hotel. He was right. And if she was completely honest with herself, the thought of going back without knowing who she was had her more than a little terrified.

But stay here? Was she crazy to consider it?

A sound drifted up to her open window. A car engine. "My driver is here," he said. "Should I send him back or have him wait for you?"

Ariel weighed her alternatives. She knew Jarrett would keep pressure on the hotel manager to find her family, so she wouldn't miss out on anything by not being at the hotel. While the man of the house might make her crazy, she liked Anna Jane. Truth be known, being here would be nicer than being alone at the hotel. Here she at least had a name, even if it wasn't her own.

"Send him back," she said, squaring her shoulders and meeting his gaze. "Thank you for inviting me. I would like to stay."

He rose to his feet.

"On one condition," she added.

He waited silently.

"Think what you want about me. I have no right to control that, but I don't want any more conversations like we had last night," she said. "If mutual respect isn't available, then I'll settle for common courtesy."

"Agreed. I'll have the boutique send over some clothes and toiletries for you. They should be here in a few hours. I'll let Leona and Anna Jane know you're our guest for the time being. Please make yourself at home."

"Thank you, Mr. Wilkenson."

"Please call me Jarrett."

"Thank you, Jarrett."

With that, he was gone. She stared after him as he moved down the stairs. What were his secrets? she wondered. What had hurt him so much that he could be generous with his things, but hold back such a large portion of himself?

"Ariel, Anna Jane, there's something here for you," Leona called.

At the sound of his housekeeper's voice, Jarrett gave up all pretense of working. He exited the spreadsheet program and returned to the main menu of his computer, then stood and walked into the foyer.

Leona stood by the open French doors and waved the two females inside. "Hurry," she said. "There's so much to see." Her hazel eyes danced with excitement. She was short and plump, with dark hair that had started graying at the temples. He'd known her for years and had, in fact, stolen her and her husband away from a business associate.

"What is it?" Anna Jane asked, scampering inside and glancing around. Her gaze fell on the pile of boxes by the front door. She squealed. "Are they for me?"

"Greedy piglet," Leona said warmly. "They're not presents, but something almost as good. Come open them with me." When Ariel started to hang back, Leona motioned her forward with a nod of her head. "There are several for you, Ariel. Come on. This will be fun."

"Are you going to watch, Uncle Jarrett?" Anna Jane asked as she dived for the boxes.

"Sure."

Ariel gave him a quick glance as she passed. No doubt she wondered what was going on. Since that morning when she'd agreed to stay at the house, she'd kept busy with Anna Jane, as if wanting to avoid him as much as possible. What she probably didn't know was that the main patio by the pool was directly outside his office. With the windows open, he could hear everything said.

At first he'd thought that was part of her plan. But as their conversation had washed over him, he'd had second thoughts. She hadn't grilled his niece about him, nor had she steered the conversation into a direction that flattered her. Instead she'd talked to Anna Jane about the girl's school and her friends. In that morning of eavesdropping Jarrett had learned more about his niece than he had in the few weeks she'd been living with him.

Was Ariel trying to use Anna Jane to get to him, or was he being paranoid? It would take a few days to figure out the truth. For now, Anna Jane wanted company and Ariel was willing to provide it. With Leona supervising the two, Anna Jane would be safe with their visitor.

Another squeal cut through his thoughts. He glanced up and saw Anna Jane opening a box of Christmas lights. "They're beautiful. Are they for a tree or decorating the house?"

"Either," he said. "The tree will be delivered in a few days."

She wrapped the long strand around her like gauze around a mummy, then ran over to him. Instinctively, he lowered himself to his knees and caught her when she flung herself toward him.

Her small body was warm and sturdy with a sweet little-girl scent that reminded him of growing up with his sister. Brown eyes glowed with happiness.

"We're getting a tree?" she asked, her voice laced with awe.

"Of course."

"You didn't forget Christmas."

He feigned a wounded expression. "Did you think I would?"

"Never!" she announced, and hugged him again.

Over her shoulder he saw Ariel watching them. He

waited, but she never hinted that while he hadn't forgotten the holiday, he'd had no intention of celebrating it until she'd reminded him that Anna Jane would expect all the trimmings.

"These are for you," Leona said to Ariel as she studied the contents of several bags. "Clothes and other things from the boutiques." She winked at Jarrett. "Looks like they didn't leave anything for the other customers."

Jarrett released his niece and stood. "I told them to send a wide selection. I guessed at the size."

Ariel pulled out a beaded cocktail dress. "The size looks right, but there's too much here."

"Take what you want and send the rest back."

"That's pretty," Anna Jane said, hurrying to her side.

"Let's get these off you before someone forgets you're a little girl and plugs you in," Leona said as she unwound the lights.

Anna Jane laughed.

Ariel joined in as she pulled more cocktail dresses from the bag. There were shoes to match, along with tiny beaded handbags. She shook her head. "Okay, this can all go back. Unless you're planning a formal event?"

"Not him," Leona answered for him. "Mr. Jarrett doesn't entertain." When he frowned, she waved away his annoyance. "It's true," she said. "You never have company. You live like a monk. You're a young man. It's not healthy."

"Leona!"

"Fine. I say too much. But it's the truth." She headed for the kitchen. "I know, I know, start lunch. I'm going."

Ariel was busy folding the evening dresses back into neat, tissue-wrapped packages. He couldn't see her face, but he suspected she was smiling at his discomfort, not to mention the housekeeper's words.

"I do not live like a monk," he growled.

"It's true," Anna Jane piped up. "Uncle Jarrett hardly ever talks to God, and monks talk to God all the time."

"Thank you," he said to his niece.

She dimpled. "You're welcome."

Ariel opened another bag. In it were shorts, shirts and a few frilly things she quickly thrust out of view. "Maybe I'll take this up to my room and sort it out there," she said.

"Don't take long," Anna Jane responded. "We have to help Leona decorate after lunch. We can do the living room and maybe wrap some lights and stuff around the banister."

"I'd like that," Ariel said. She scooped up an armful of clothing and rose to her feet. "Gee, Jarrett, you'd better hope that in my other life I'm frugal, so I have a lot of room left on my credit cards. Everything is very beautiful and it's going to be tough for me to decide what I want. I might end up picking several things."

He stared at her. "You expect to pay me back?"

"Of course. Why wouldn't I?"

Because he was rich and no one ever tried to pay him back. Most people made it a habit to see how much they could get from him. Ariel stepped close and lowered her voice.

"I don't know who your friends are, but you might want to think about hanging out with some different kinds of people. I swear, even if I'm working somewhere for minimum wage, I'll pay you for these. It might take a while, but I'll do it."

Conviction burned in her green eyes. He figured even odds that she was lying...about everything else. He believed her about the clothes and her wanting to pay him back.

She climbed the stairs, her shorts showing off long, shapely legs. His reaction was as quick as it was predictable. Leona was right; he'd been living like a monk for too long. Yet there wasn't a damn thing he could do about it. He, of all people, knew the risk of getting involved.

Chapter Five

Ariel hung her new clothes in the spacious closet. Anna Jane curled up on the queen-size mattress and watched her. "It's funny to have the weather so nice," the nine-year-old said.

Ariel glanced at her over her shoulder. She still wore her hair in a pretty French braid. Anna Jane fingered her own short hair and wondered how long it would take to grow it enough to braid. She'd wanted it long, but her mother had always said it was too much work. Maybe she should talk to Uncle Jarrett. She didn't think he would mind how she wore her hair.

"Where are you from?" Ariel asked.

"Manhattan. We wouldn't always have snow for Christmas, but it was usually cold. Here it's warm all the time."

"I know what you mean. I keep expecting a little whiff of something chilly." Ariel frowned.

"Do you remember where you're from?" Anna Jane asked eagerly.

"Not exactly. I can picture fog and rain. But nothing specific, which means it's not much help. It gets foggy and rainy just about everywhere."

"Not here."

Ariel grinned. "That's right. Not here. Every day is a good-hair day on St. Alicia." She sat on the edge of the bed and started folding T-shirts.

The clothes she'd chosen were different from what Anna Jane's mother would wear. The casual shorts and shirts, along with a few dresses, wouldn't suit her mother's designer tastes. But Anna Jane liked them. It was important to dress up in the city, but here it didn't matter.

"Do you miss New York?" Ariel asked.

"Some. My school."

"Friends?"

Anna Jane wrinkled her nose. "I'd changed schools in September so I hadn't made a lot of friends, but I miss the classes and the teachers."

Ariel put down the shirt she'd been folding and reached forward, resting her hand on Anna Jane's bare knee. "It's tough being the new kid, huh?"

"Yeah. Some of the girls talked to me, but most of them were real snobs."

"And really stupid," Ariel said, giving her a quick squeeze before returning to her folding. "You're a great kid and they were too dumb to figure that out. Hey, if they'd taken the time to get to know you, they could have visited you here. It's their loss."

"I hadn't thought of it that way." Her comments made Anna Jane feel better. It was funny. On the outside Ariel and Nana B. didn't look anything alike. Her nanny had been nearly sixty and tiny, with white hair and snapping black eyes. Yet Ariel reminded her of Nana B. It was more what she said.

"Do you have any children?" Anna Jane asked.

Ariel glanced at her and opened her mouth. She frowned. "I'm not sure."

Anna Jane rolled her eyes. "I keep forgetting you don't remember who you are. I'll try not to ask so many questions."

"I don't mind the questions. There's stuff I don't realize I know until I answer. But children. How strange." She got up and put her shirts and shorts into the dresser at the foot of the bed, then returned to her seat. "My first instinct was to say that I don't have children, but then I wanted to say yes." She tilted her head as she thought. "I don't think I have any of my own, but there are kids in my life."

"Like friends?"

"Maybe. Or kids of friends. Maybe nieces and nephews. I'm not sure."

Anna Jane realized she didn't want Ariel to have other children in her life. She wanted to be the only one. Which was silly. After lunch Leona had explained to her that Ariel was just here temporarily. Anna Jane knew that. Yet part of her didn't want to believe it. Part of her wanted to pretend that Ariel was going to be here for a long time.

She wanted Ariel to love her the way Nana B. had loved her. She wanted to belong to someone. Her mother had belonged to her father. Uncle Jarrett belonged to his empire. Anna Jane didn't belong to anyone or anything. Belonging to Ariel would be very nice.

Ariel looked at the pretty young girl sitting so quietly on the bed. "You're looking serious about something," she teased. "Tell me what it is."

"Nothing," came the quiet response.

It was definitely something, Ariel thought, trying to read Anna Jane's expression. Unfortunately she'd inherited the Wilkenson ability to hide what she was thinking.

"There are still a couple of hours until dinner. Maybe we could do something."

Shrug.

"Do you want to play a game?"

Shrug number two, this one accompanied by a small hand picking at the bedspread.

"How about exploring the house? I haven't seen very much of it. It's big enough that we could even pretend to get lost and have Leona come look for us."

Silence. Ariel replayed their conversation. They'd talked about Anna Jane not fitting in at school and her, Ariel, not being sure if she had children. Bingo!

She scooted up until she was sitting next to Anna Jane, then draped her arm around her shoulders. "You miss your mother, don't you?"

Anna Jane raised her head. Tears filled her eyes, then one slipped down her cheek. The young girl slowly shook her head. "No," she whispered. "I'm very bad."

Ariel's heart ached for the child. "Honey, you're a lot of things, but bad isn't one of them. Tell me what's wrong."

"I can't. You won't like me."

"Unless you plan on selling me to pirates or burning down the house, I can't think of anything you could do that would make me not like you." She gave the girl a gentle shake. "Come on. Out with it. I promise I'm not easily shocked."

Anna Jane swallowed hard. "My mom died."

She clamped her lips shut. Ariel resisted the urge to ask more questions. A voice inside her head whispered it would be better to wait. Almost as if she'd been through a similar experience herself. Had she?

Forget it, she scolded, pushing aside her questions. Her past wasn't important right now. She focused on the child and waited.

"I miss her," Anna Jane continued in a halting voice. "Sort of. But not like I miss Nana B."

"She was your former nanny?" Ariel asked, taking a guess.

"Uh-huh." More tears fell. Anna Jane wiped them away. "She retired in September when I went to the new school. She lives with her sister. I miss her so much." She covered her mouth to hold back a sob.

"Oh, honey, of course you miss her. She was there for you every day. I know she misses you, too." Without thinking, she pulled Anna Jane close and rocked her. "I've never had a nanny—at least, I can't remember having one, but I understand it can be a very special relationship. This is so hard for you, losing your nanny and your mother within a few months. No wonder you wanted a friend."

"They asked her to come back," Anna Jane said, then hiccuped. Small hands clung to Ariel, holding tight as if the child would never let go. "I heard them. But her sister had fallen and broken her hip, so Nana B. couldn't get away. But I wanted her to come back."

"I know." Ariel had to blink several times to hold in her own tears. She continued to rock the grieving child, smoothing her hair and rubbing her back. "You love her and miss her. Sometimes you're afraid because you think loving her so much is wrong. But it's never wrong to love someone."

"But I love her more than Mommy. That's wrong."

At last. The heart of the problem. She inhaled the scent

of little girl and felt the heat of her small body. There was something familiar about the moment. The whisper of a memory teased at her, but she couldn't bring it close enough to grab it.

"There is no less or more in love. There's also no wrong in giving with a full heart. You loved them differently because they had different places in your life. Nana B. shared the little moments of your life. We live in little moments, so we tend to remember them better and miss them more because there are more of them to miss." She frowned. "Did that make sense?"

Anna Jane sniffed. "Uh-huh."

"Good. So some days you really miss Nana B. and I bet there are some days you really miss your mom. Never think it's wrong to miss someone or love someone who cares about you. Love is the best part of who we are."

Ariel had no idea where her advice was coming from, but Anna Jane seemed comforted by it, so who was she to question herself?

"I'm scared," Anna Jane said.

"Why?"

"What if they send me away? I heard the lawyer talking about that. About boarding school." She raised her chin and met Ariel's gaze. "But if Uncle Jarrett dies and I'm all alone, I'll be poor and have to live in the attic, just like Sara Crewe. In *The Little Princess,*" she added, obviously reading Ariel's confusion.

Ariel remembered the story. "That's not going to happen." She hugged the girl close. "Your uncle is very rich and he's not going to lose his money, so don't you worry about living in an attic."

"But what about boarding school?"

"I'll talk to him," Ariel promised, then wondered what on earth she was saying. Jarrett wasn't a real fan of hers and wouldn't take kindly to any parenting advice she had to offer. Still, this was about his niece, not him. He would just have to get over it.

She wondered if she would feel so brave when she actually faced the lion in his den.

At Anna Jane's hopeful expression she added, "I'll make sure he understands. It's going to be fine. You'll see."

"Thank you." Anna Jane rested her head on her shoulder. "I'm glad you were the one who found my bottle."

"Me, too," Ariel responded, sincere despite all that had happened and the potential for disaster in the future. "So how about a tour of the house?"

"Okay." The nine-year-old bounced off the bed and wiped away the last traces of her tears. "It's really big. There are six bedrooms and even a telescope up in a little room in the attic."

"Sounds great. Think we'll need to bring a compass?" Anna Jane laughed. "I can find our way back."

"You sure? We could ask Leona for bread crumbs. Of course, she'd probably want us to vacuum them up on our way back and I don't want to lug a big vacuum cleaner with us on our travels, do you?"

"You're weird."

"I know. Isn't it great?"

Still laughing, Anna Jane led the way out of Ariel's room. As she followed the child, she tried to figure out why making friends with the girl was so easy. Had she been a nanny to some wealthy family? Was she a teacher? Maybe she worked in a pediatrician's office as a nurse or physician's assistant.

Anything was possible.

She decided to dwell on the questions later. For now she would enjoy the tour of Jarrett's beautiful home.

They started at the top and worked their way down. As promised, a small widow's walk led to a protected room containing large windows and an expensive-looking telescope. On the next floor were smaller bedrooms and a large game room complete with a pool table and big-screen television.

The second floor held the remaining bedrooms, including Anna Jane's and Ariel's, and Jarrett's. Ariel didn't go into that room, not wanting to intrude. Somehow the thought of seeing where Jarrett slept unnerved her. If possible, she wanted to keep the image of tangled sheets and the man himself very separate in her mind.

At the end of the hall, double French doors led to what looked like an exercise studio. "There's weights and stuff," Anna Jane said knowledgeably. "Uncle Jarrett is very strong."

"So I've noticed." She pushed open the door. As she did, she heard the low rumble of a motor, along with a rhythmic thudding of feet. She turned in that direction and saw Jarrett on the treadmill.

A television mounted on the wall was turned to CNN. He faced away from the door and so far hadn't noticed their interruption. Ariel told herself to back out before they were spotted, but her feet didn't obey the command.

So she watched him, watched the steady movements of his body. Powerful arms pumped back and forth. Long legs strode easily. He wore shorts and a cropped T-shirt that exposed his midsection. His back was broad and tanned. Sweat formed a V down the faded gray shirt.

Unable to help herself, she allowed her gaze to drift to the mirror in front of him...the mirror that reflected his image perfectly. Those long legs and taut thighs were just as alluring from the front. His belly was a hard, ridged plane of muscle, his shoulders impossibly wide. Even his face held strength and power.

He moved with the grace of a wild animal, and something unknown and primitive inside her responded. She tried to ignore the heat—the desire swelling and rising like a wave headed for shore. She *couldn't* be attracted to him. Anyone but him. For one thing, he didn't trust her. For another, she didn't know if she was worth trusting. She wanted to think so; she believed so with all her heart, but she wasn't *sure*. She couldn't *be* sure until her memory returned. Regardless of her past, Jarrett was the kind of man who was trouble. Safe enough to admire from afar. Better yet, to not notice at all.

Neither she nor Anna Jane made a sound, yet he stiffened suddenly and shifted his gaze from the television to the mirror. Their gazes locked.

Something sparked between them. Fire, maybe. Or need. The sensation was unfamiliar but powerful. She felt herself drawn to him. Images of them together, wrapped in an intimate embrace, filled her mind. Her hands ached to touch his skin; her body heated at the thought of being caressed by him, of being claimed by his strength.

And then it was gone. She wasn't sure who blinked first, or if there'd been a distinct shift in the cosmos, but suddenly the connection was broken. She struggled to catch her breath, wondering if she'd imagined the moment, if his hard breathing was only the result of his time on the treadmill.

Anna Jane noticed he'd caught sight of them. "Uncle Jarrett, I'm taking Ariel on a tour of the house," she said importantly.

"Have a good time," he said.

"We are. When's the Christmas tree coming?"

A smile tugged at the corners of his mouth. "Soon."

"But it's almost Christmas."

"Not for just over a week. Don't worry. It will be here in time."

Anna Jane looked doubtful, but she trusted her uncle enough not to question him further. She wrinkled her nose. "You're all sweaty, Uncle Jarrett. Why do you run like that?"

"It's good for my heart."

It was also excellent for the rest of him, Ariel thought, still impressed by his physique. Her strange circumstances were keeping her up nights. It looked as if she would lie awake tonight for a completely different and potentially more dangerous reason.

He was getting better at shutting out the distractions, Jarrett told himself, hoping if he said it enough it might just come true.

Even with his office door closed, he heard muffled conversation and laughter. Whatever the reason Ariel had first shown up in his life, he couldn't regret what she was doing with Anna Jane. The past three days had transformed the child. Instead of being quiet and keeping to the background, she'd started living life again, speaking up and having fun. It was what he wanted for her. What he didn't like was that someone else had been the one to make it happen.

They still hadn't solved the mystery that was Ariel. No one had come forward to report her missing. Not on St. Alicia or any of the nearby islands. She'd stopped looking up hopefully every time he walked into the room. As if she'd decided there wasn't going to be a rescue from this particular situation.

To make things worse, Jarrett still hadn't come to terms with his feelings about the woman. Was she genuine or was she toying with him? There didn't seem to be an easy answer to that question. Nor was he going to find one today, he reminded himself. But he did have a report to finish.

He returned his attention to the spreadsheet in front of him. The numbers were momentarily meaningless as he strained to listen to the sudden and surprising silence in the foyer. Perhaps Ariel and Anna Jane had gone out to the beach. His window had a hundred-and-eighty-degree view of the ocean. He could glance up and see if they were there. If she was wearing a bathing suit. Something that left her long legs bare and her—

Stop it! he commanded himself silently. No more interruptions. He would concentrate on work.

Slowly he lost himself in his report, compiling numbers, determining trends at the seven newest Wilkenson hotels. His corporate accounts were increasing. The weekend specials to bring in local business had been more successful than projected. He made a note to review the cost-benefit ratios and—

Something brushed against his arm. He swatted away the offending creature and tapped a couple of keys. The computer program scrolled to the end of the spreadsheet. He studied the summary figures.

The tickling came again. As he absently pulled his arm closer to his body, he inhaled the scent of pine. At the same moment he registered that he wasn't alone in his office.

Ariel giggled as he turned to glance at her. She stood next to his chair, a small pine branch in her hands. She brushed it against his arm again. "You have amazing concentration," she said.

"Thank you," he answered, wondering what she would think if he told her exactly how often he lost his concentration because he was thinking about her. She wasn't wearing the bathing suit he'd fantasized about a few moments before. Instead, a red T-shirt had been tucked into white shorts, but he wasn't about to complain. He still had a perfect view of long legs and bare arms. The soft T-shirt material hugged her breasts, making his palms ache to cup her sweet curves. Today her hair was loose, a riot of gold-blond curls tumbling over her shoulders and down her back. So far she hadn't worn her hair the same way twice. He'd overheard Anna Jane asking about that. Ariel had replied that she couldn't figure out how she usually wore her hair, so she was experimenting until something felt right.

"Your presence is requested," she said, waving the branch in front of him. "As you may have guessed, the Christmas tree has been delivered." She grinned. "This is the tropics, Jarrett. Did you have to have it flown in especially?"

"There wasn't much choice."

"Well, they sent you a fabulous tree. It's huge. Frank had to cut it to make it fit in the living room. We talked about putting it in the foyer, but that's not very cozy and familylike. The living room is better. At least, that was my opinion. Hope you don't mind."

"I hadn't thought about it one way or the other."

"Typical," she said, heading for the door. "But we forgive you. Come on. You need to help decorate."

"I have to work."

She stopped and faced him. Wide green eyes filled with amusement. "Didn't we already talk about those ghosts, Ebenezer? Aren't you the least bit worried about facing them?"

He couldn't resist her smile. "Are you always like this?"

She sniffed the pine branch in her arms. "Like what?"

"Impulsive. Interrupting people's work days to do things like decorate for the holidays."

Her smile faded. "I don't know, but I hope so. I'd hate to be any other way. Besides, impulsive beats stuffy."

"Are you calling me stuffy?"

"Are you going to help decorate?"

"Yes."

"Then you're not stuffy. At least, not for now."

"Gee, thanks."

She dimpled. "You're welcome."

He followed her into the foyer. A trail of pine needles led them to the living room. "Remind me not to negotiate with you about anything. You're too fond of conditional clauses."

"Everything in life is conditional," Ariel said, tossing her head. Afternoon sunlight caught her curls and turned them to the color of spun gold. "Well, not love, of course, but everything else." She stepped into the living room. "He's here. I told you I could persuade him."

Anna Jane raced toward him and wrapped her arms around his waist as she hugged him. "Uncle Jarrett, we're decorating the tree and I'm giving instructions. Isn't it beautiful? It's so big. We had to cut off some to make it fit." She pointed to a pile of branches stacked by the doorway. "Frank trimmed those off and Ariel's gonna decorate with them and doesn't it smell just like Christmas?"

He ruffled her bangs, then touched her cheek with the back of his fingers. Smiling at him like that, she reminded him of his sister. Tracy had always loved the holidays, or anytime when she might get presents.

Anna Jane didn't wait for him to respond to her comments. Instead she ran back to the tree and watched anxiously as Frank strung lights.

The two white sofas and green print wing chairs had already been pushed back to make room. The tree stood in the center of the large bay window overlooking the ocean. Its top was less than six inches from the twelve-foot ceiling. Leona had already opened several boxes of decorations.

The unfamiliar scene made him think about the empty places in his life. Ariel had spoken about unconditional love, but Jarrett had never experienced that particular emotion. Tracy had. His sister had loved her husband to the exclusion of the rest of the world. Unfortunately, that had left her only child on the outside looking in. He cared about his sister, but he hadn't been blind to her faults. Even her husband's death hadn't been enough to remind her of Anna Jane's needs.

He never understood Tracy's obsession with Donald. He still didn't. How had she known he was the one? Why had she been willing to risk so much? He'd always thought of her as weak, yet loving like that took a strength he couldn't begin to muster.

His niece laughed. He smiled at the sound.

"Are we amusing you?" Ariel asked as she paused by him on her way to get more pine branches. She'd already placed several above the fireplace. The dark green contrasted with the white walls and marble floor and mantel.

"I like the sound of Anna Jane's laugher. I was thinking that I don't hear it enough."

"I'm not surprised. She's been through a lot. You're lucky that she's as well-adjusted as she is."

He wanted to question how she could know if Anna Jane was well-adjusted, but this wasn't the time to pursue

Ariel's supposed lack of memory. "I don't know what to do with her."

"It's easy." Ariel handed him several branches. "Just love her and be there for her. The rest of it sort of takes care of itself."

"You're oversimplifying. Parenting is a difficult responsibility."

"Some people would say the same thing about running a business."

He grimaced. "Not bringing in a profit and destroying a child's life aren't the same thing."

"You're going to be fine, Jarrett. If you're this concerned, there's no way you'll mess up badly enough to destroy Anna Jane's life." She bent over and grabbed another armful of branches. "I can't get over this. It's December, we're decorating for Christmas and I'm in shorts. Too weird."

"There's not even a hint of snow."

She frowned. "I don't think I expect snow. I'm not sure." She shook her head. "A word of advice. Don't lose your memory. It'll make you crazy."

She was already making him crazy. Did she know? Was it part of her plan? "If you don't expect snow, what do you want?"

"Something wonderful."

Their gazes locked. He remembered her watching him run on the treadmill and the emotions he'd seen in her eyes. Had he read desire, or had he simply projected what he wanted to see? The hell of it was, he almost didn't care. After all, the situation was already impossible. He was attracted to a woman he didn't trust. That was pretty typical of the disasters that had passed for relationships in his life.

Ariel leaned close. "Have you bought Anna Jane any presents?"

"I've sent away for a few things."

"Like what?"

He tried to remember, but all he could see was Ariel standing in front of him. It didn't take a whole lot of imagination to picture her naked, beneath him, sighing with pleasure as he—

"Uh, I don't recall," he said, then cleared his throat. "What would you suggest?"

"Books, a computer, some learning software, maybe a few games. Dolls, but maybe not, because she's pretty mature. A stuffed animal or two. Oh, and a puppy or kitten. You know, something for her to love." She tilted her head. "That's a good starting place. But don't get too wild. You don't want to spoil her."

He stared at her. "You want me to buy her all that, then tell me not to spoil her? Make up your mind."

Ariel laughed. "Okay, maybe I got carried away. But you get the idea."

"Yeah, right." He chuckled.

Instantly she stiffened. Startled, he glanced around the room and realized everyone was looking at him. "What's wrong?" he asked.

"Nothing," Leona said, returning her attention to the decorations.

"You were laughing, Uncle Jarrett," Anna Jane said. "I've never heard you laugh before. It sounds nice."

Chapter Six

Jarrett closed the book and set it on Anna Jane's nightstand. She gazed up at him and sighed. "That was a great story. Are we going to start a new one tomorrow?"

"Sure. You have one picked out?"

"Of course."

Her sweet grin touched his old, battered heart, stirring the rusty organ to life. He hadn't thought he would ever care about anyone, but it was surprisingly simple to love this child. Maybe being her guardian was going to be easier than he'd first thought.

He bent close and kissed her cheek. "I figured as much. Now go to sleep."

She touched his arm. "Uncle Jarrett, has anyone called about Ariel?"

He thought about his daily talks with his hotel manager. So far there had been no word. He shook his head. "Not yet."

"I know she's sad about it," Anna Jane said. "She's sad because she thinks no one wants her."

"I'm sure she has family and friends somewhere. They just don't know that she's missing." He knew that had to be true. A woman like her couldn't exist in a vacuum.

"But what if she doesn't? What will happen to her?"

The possibility existed that her friends knew exactly where she was and what she was doing. That would be true if she'd come to St. Alicia with the express desire to get in touch with him. But he didn't share that possibility with Anna Jane. Not only because he didn't want to upset her, but because in the past couple of days he'd become less sure what he believed about their mysterious visitor.

"She'll figure something out," he told his niece. "Don't worry."

"If she doesn't have any family, can we keep her?"

"She's not a stray puppy. We can't ask her to stay."

Anna Jane laughed. "That's what Ariel said. Why can't we ask her to stay? She likes it here. She likes us and we like her." She wrinkled her nose. "Well, *I* like her, but sometimes I don't think you do."

"I like her just fine," he said, barely acknowledging the lie. He had a lot of conflicting feelings for Ariel, and none of them involved "like." Now, if his niece had asked about want—that he could have answered.

"You don't like her the way Mommy liked Daddy."

"No. Your parents had a very special love." One he wasn't sure he could believe in. And even if he was willing to believe, he wasn't sure he was willing to take a chance on it.

"Mommy and Daddy loved each other more than they loved me," Anna Jane said, her voice matter-of-fact.

Jarrett glanced at her sharply. Her face was calm, without a hint of pain. "Why do you say that?"

"Because it's true. Nana B. told me that it was better that way. That mommies and daddies are supposed to love each other more than they love their children. One day the children are going to grow up and leave and the parents are left with each other. So they have to love each other more."

Her voice had grown wistful with the telling. Jarrett knew enough to read between the lines. Anna Jane didn't object to her parents loving each other more, but she wished there had been something left over for her.

He brushed the bangs from her forehead and wondered what it must have been like when Anna Jane had lost first her nanny, then her mother. Her entire world had been turned upside down. Then she'd found herself here—on a strange island with a man she didn't know. How was he going to make it all right with her?

"Ariel's very nice," she said.

"Are you matchmaking?"

Anna Jane smiled. "What's that?"

"You don't fool me, kid. You have the vocabulary of a forty-year-old, so don't pretend you don't understand me. I've told you. Ariel has her own life, and when she gets her memory back—" or he figured out who she was "—she's going to return to where she belongs. That's how it has to be."

Anna Jane nodded slowly. "But she's here for now, right?"

"Right." He kissed her cheek. "Now go to sleep."

He turned out the light on the nightstand and left the room. As he walked to his office, he thought about Anna Jane's question. What if no one came looking for Ariel? He told himself eventually someone would. Or, assuming she was faking it, when she figured out he wasn't going to fall for her, she would leave on her own.

But he didn't like the thought of her faking it as much as he once had. There was a part of him that wanted to trust her. He told himself it was because she was spending so much time with his niece. He didn't want the child influenced by a liar. Yet he knew in his heart *he* was the liar. He wanted Ariel to be who she claimed because he couldn't stop wanting her.

"Hell," he muttered as he went down the stairs and crossed to his office. He had it bad. There was only one solution, and that was work.

As he entered the room, his fingers paused by the light switch, but he didn't touch it. A flicker of movement outside the window caught his attention instead.

He walked toward his desk. With the subtle illumination from the pool and from the patio, he could make out a familiar shape. Ariel sat on the low stone wall that separated the pool area from the beach. There was something about the way she'd pulled her knees up to her chest and wrapped her arms around her legs. She had her back to his office, so he couldn't see her face, but he sensed she was upset.

Without considering that he was already in over his head, he moved quickly through the downstairs, circling through rooms and finally exiting by the kitchen. He cut across the path and onto the grass where the thick growth would muffle the sound of his footsteps.

He walked up behind her. In the distance, night creatures called to each other. Waves broke gently on the sand. "Enjoying the view?" he asked.

She jumped slightly, then lowered her legs to the sand and quickly wiped her face. Had she been crying? The thought of her tears caught him like a punch to the gut.

"It's a beautiful night," she said, her voice husky. She was still wearing what she'd had on at dinner. A bright green silky tank top with a ridiculously large parrot pin by her shoulder. Her skirt was long and nearly reached to her ankles. She was anything but sophisticated. She wasn't like the cool, remote beauties he was used to, yet he had a nearly overwhelming urge to take her in his arms.

"Are you waiting for the stars to come out?" he asked.

"Not really. I—" She shivered. "I'm sorry, Jarrett, but I'm not very good company tonight. I know as a guest part of my responsibility is to be witty and entertaining. Would you settle for a rain check?"

Just when he thought he had her nearly figured out, she surprised him. She was trying to chase him off. Not exactly the actions of a woman determined to get her hooks into a man. Was he wrong abut her? Was it possible the situation was as simple as she said—that she'd just lost her memory? Would it be safe to believe her?

He drew in a breath. He knew the price of trusting someone and being wrong. He knew the results could be fatal.

"I don't need to be entertained," he said, and moved to the sea wall and sat next to her. Maybe he could let go enough to talk about something safe. "Although I would like to discuss my niece for a minute, if you don't mind."

"Anna Jane? Is she all right?"

"Yes. I just left her and she's fine. I was reading her a story before tucking her into bed. I worry she's a little old for that, but I guess it's not a bad habit."

Ariel glanced at him. Her long curly hair had been pulled back into a ponytail, exposing her face. Light from the kitchen window illuminated the right side, while the left was in shadow. She was incredibly beautiful.

"I'll admit Anna Jane seems a little grown up to want to be read to, but I don't think this is about the story. She just wants contact with you. It's your special time together and she treasures that."

"I hadn't thought of that. I worry about her. This is so strange for her. She's had to leave everything behind. Her school, her friends. It would have been easier if her former nanny had been able to accompany her, but that wasn't possible."

"Anna Jane mentioned that to me," Ariel said. "Something about a medical problem in the family."

"Exactly." He stretched his legs out in front of him and crossed his feet at the ankles. "Those two were very close. Not that the situation would have been much better if Tracy hadn't used a nanny. After all, Anna Jane lost her, too."

"Tracy is your sister?"

"Yes."

"I'm in an awkward position," Ariel said. When he glanced at her, she shrugged. "Your niece told me a couple of things a few days ago. She didn't ask me to keep them confidential and I don't think she would mind me telling you, but I feel funny about it."

"Do you want me to force it from you?"

Ariel smiled. "No, but thanks for asking. I guess I'm saying I'd like you to keep me out of any discussion you have with her about this. I don't want her to feel I'm ratting on her behind her back, or that she can't trust me."

Again she surprised him. Her obvious concern for Anna Jane didn't fit with the personality of a gold digger. "I'll be diplomatic," he promised.

Ariel nodded. "I'm going to have to trust that you know how. I guess you must, if you can run a business successfully enough that you live here. Anyway, Anna Jane is feeling very guilty. She misses her nanny more than she misses her mother, and she believes that's wrong."

"The poor kid," he said. "What did you tell her?"

"That her reaction was normal. It's okay to love more than one person. I tried to explain that she and her nanny had shared day-to-day moments, so it made sense she would miss those more than special occasions with her mother."

"Did she understand?"

"I hope so, but I'm not sure."

Jarrett rubbed his temple. "Just when I think Tracy made the right decision in leaving her daughter with me, something like this happens and I know I'm going to mess her up without meaning to. I have no training at parenting."

"Neither do most first-time parents."

"Yeah, but at least they start out with an infant. I've got a little person sleeping up there and I don't know what to do with her."

"Love her, Jarrett. Maybe you could talk about her mother and Nana B. and try to explain it to her again, so she knows it's okay."

"That's a good idea." He drew in a breath and smelled the salty spray from the sea. While he didn't have to explain, a part of him felt obligated to make Ariel understand the unique relationship Tracy and her husband had shared. "Tracy and Donald weren't like most couples."

"In what way?"

"They loved each other to the exclusion of the rest of

the world. When it was just the two of them, that was fine, but once Anna Jane came along, they still weren't willing to come up for air. Then Donald was killed in a car accident. Tracy never recovered. In a way, Anna Jane has been an orphan since birth.''

"At least she had Nana B.''

"You're right. Nana B. loved her as if she were one of her own children. That stability got Anna Jane through.''

They sat in silence for a few minutes. Ariel turned toward him, resting one knee on the wall and tucking that foot under her opposite leg. "Have you ever loved anyone like that?'' she asked.

"No. Have you?''

She shook her head, then paused. "No, I haven't. I'm sure of it. Of all the things I had to remember, why was it that?'' She gave him a forced smile. "I would rather remember a great love I'd lost than to have never loved anyone. What a sad statement on my life. Don't you think?''

"It sounds more sensible than sad, if you ask me.''

"Sensible? So you don't believe in love?''

"I think it's overrated.'' Again his mind drifted to Charlotte. She'd been on his mind a lot these past few days. Something about these circumstances, he supposed, hoping she would again become a distant memory very soon. Whatever lesson he might have wanted to learn from his sister's one true love had been negated by the reality of Charlotte's destruction.

"Do you still think I'm lying?'' Ariel asked unexpectedly.

He looked at her, at the curve of her cheek and the fullness of her mouth, at the bruises that had nearly faded. "Are you?''

"You ask that question so easily, as if you're actually willing to believe my answer." She sighed. "I'm not lying. I have no reason to lie."

"I have no reason to believe you."

"Okay, I'll bite. Why won't you believe me?"

He glanced back at the sea, a dark, murky mystery blending with the horizon until it was impossible to see where one ended and the other began.

"It's a long, ugly story," he said.

"I'm willing to listen if you're willing to tell it."

He understood that by simply offering her the truth, he'd already made a decision of sorts. On some level he *was* willing to trust her. Dear God, don't let him be wrong again.

"My parents died when I was eighteen," he began, blocking out the view in front of him and instead staring into the past. "I don't remember much about that time except it rained during the funeral and that it was unusually cold for August. Tracy was already in college and I was due to start in a few weeks. The Wilkenson family has been in hotels since they came over from England in the early 1800s. In nearly two hundred years fortunes had been made and lost. Fourteen years ago we were in one of the bad times."

He spoke the words without thinking, almost as if he'd told this tale a thousand times before. But the truth was, he'd never told it. Business associates learned bits and pieces from rumors and gossip. He'd discussed specific areas of his past when they were relevant to his work, but that wasn't often.

"Things have changed," Ariel said. "You're obviously very successful."

He shrugged. His ability to turn the company around wasn't the point. "I finished college in three years so I could get right to work," he went on. "For a while there was talk of Tracy taking over instead, but she was never interested and once she met Donald, she didn't want to spend time working. It took me five years to get the company back on its feet."

"Let me guess," she said softly. "You worked twenty-hour days and never came up for air."

"Exactly." He turned toward her. "I didn't have time for anything else. Then, when I finally could draw a breath, I realized the world had taken notice of me and everyone wanted a piece of the Wilkenson genius." He grimaced. "It was hell."

"Even the women?" she teased.

Her question shocked him, then he remembered she didn't know the truth about what had happened. "Let's just say there were downsides to that. I was emotionally still a kid. My college class load hadn't left a lot of time for socializing, and neither had my work schedule. I wasn't prepared to be that popular. In the end, I withdrew so I could stay whole."

"Is that why you moved here?"

He nodded.

"You're so cut off from everything. Doesn't that bother you?"

"I prefer to think of it as one long vacation." He didn't have a choice. He couldn't go back. But he was lying about the vacation. He recognized his home on St. Alicia for what it was—a very beautiful, very secure prison.

"You're trapped here," she said, surprising him by reading between the lines. "Are you staying because you want to or because you don't have a choice?"

"Both," he admitted.

She tucked a loose hair behind her ear. "What about Anna Jane? You can't keep her here forever."

"I know. I've thought about sending her back to the States. Maybe to a good boarding school."

"She's already afraid of that," Ariel told him. "Are you familiar with a children's book called *The Little Princess?*"

He shook his head.

"Anna Jane has read it several times. The story is about a young girl who is sent to boarding school in England while her father stays in India, searching for his fortune. She has beautiful clothes and is treated like a little princess. Then her father dies and she's left penniless, until her guardian finally finds her. Actually, she finds him, but that's not the point. Anna Jane is worried that if she goes to boarding school you're going to die and she's going to be penniless and forced to live in an attic."

"That's not going to happen."

"She's only nine, so don't expect her to believe you right off. We're not talking about logic. This fear is based on the fact that everyone she's ever cared about has left her. This isn't about being poor, but being abandoned. It's going to take time for her to trust caring again."

So he and his niece had something in common. Yet he wanted more for her than the solitary existence he was forced to endure.

"She needs an education," he said. "What's the solution? There's a day school on a neighboring island, but she would have to board at least during the week. I suppose I could hire tutors."

"I think you should talk to her," Ariel told him. "You can't separate her from other children, and you can't let her think she's been abandoned."

Returning to the States was an obvious solution, but not an option.

"You know a lot about children," he said.

"Isn't it odd? I've been thinking about it and I can't explain it. Maybe I'm a child psychologist or a teacher. I hate not knowing things about myself. I've been trying to define my life, so I started making a list."

"Tell me what you have so far."

She raised her eyebrows. "I'm not feeling that strong, Jarrett."

"You're afraid I'll insult you?"

"Let's just say you're not my biggest fan."

She *did* have a point, he conceded. "I won't say anything unkind."

"Ooh, there's a promise to make a girl's heart beat faster." She straightened. "Okay, but no wisecracks." She pulled a piece of paper out of her pocket and tilted it so it faced the light from the kitchen. "I have something to do with children, but young children, not teenagers. I have no sense of dealing with them." She grinned. "So I must be intelligent."

He laughed. "You have a point."

She returned her attention to the list. "I like reading. When I went through your library, I realized I've read a lot of the books there. I can remember the plots. I enjoy mysteries and romances, which, by the way, your library is sadly lacking."

"So noted. Go on."

"That's about it. I have a sense of humor and—" She bit her lower lip and folded the paper. "That's me. A few lines on a page and not much else. I would expect to have more to show for myself."

Her mood had shifted like the tide. Where before she'd been accessible, moving toward him, now she retreated, pulling into herself. Her shoulders hunched forward. "I can't believe there isn't a single person looking for me. That feels so wrong and empty. People can't live like that, can they? There has to be someone, somewhere."

She shuddered and turned her back. He reached out a hand to touch her, then let it fall to the wall. He had no right to comfort her...and no comfort to offer. "We'll find your family," he said, feeling awkward, knowing the words weren't enough.

"What if you can't? What if they don't exist?" Her voice cracked. "I'm sorry," she whispered, and stood. "I need to be alone now."

She headed for the water. Without thinking, Jarrett followed her. "Ariel, wait."

She shook her head and kept walking. He caught her in three long strides. "Ariel," he said as he took her arm and turned her toward him.

Tears flowed silently down her cheeks. Not knowing what else to do, he pulled her close and held her.

"Why are you being n-nice to me?" she asked, clinging to him and pressing her face into the crook of his neck. "You don't even like me."

Hot, wet tears splashed onto his shirt. "I don't dislike you."

Her burst of laughter turned into a strangled sob. "Be careful, Jarrett. Compliments like that will go to my head."

"I don't know what to believe," he said, surprised to find it was the truth. "You're hurting and I want to make it better. This is all I know how to do."

She sniffed and raised her head to look at him. "You do it well."

He kept one hand on the small of her back and wiped her face with the other. "Thanks."

Ariel didn't know what was worse. The confusion that was her life, or the rightness she felt in Jarrett's arms. They had nothing in common; the best he could say about her was that he didn't dislike her. A relationship between them would be insane. Yet for the first time since losing her memory, she wasn't afraid. Somehow his strength chased the demons away.

She told herself that all she felt was physical attraction. That explained the heat in her body and her desire to melt into him until they became one being. But attraction didn't explain why she felt as if this was where she belonged. What if there was someone waiting for her? What if she was already in love with someone else?

But she wasn't. She would have bet her soul on the fact. So she willed him to keep on holding her.

The tide tickled her toes. His arms continued to make her feel safe. While they'd been talking, the moon had risen above the horizon, bathing Jarrett in an unearthly glow. He looked powerful and forbidding. And incredibly beautiful.

"You are so beautiful," he said, stroking her cheek with the back of his hand.

She laughed. "That's what I was thinking about you. I hate that you read my mind."

"Is that what I do?"

Was he moving closer, or was she? Did it matter? "You do more than that," she murmured. "You—"

The brush of his mouth against hers silenced her. They'd been moving toward this moment since he'd taken her in his arms, and still she was shocked by the pressure of his lips.

He didn't move, didn't push or urge. Instead he held her and touched her...as if she were precious and special and someone he'd waited his whole life to find. The sense of homecoming had her fighting tears. She clutched at his shoulders, not daring to let go in case he disappeared from her life as quickly as he'd arrived.

It was a perfect moment. The kind that occurs only a handful of times in a single life. She wasn't sure how long they stood there like that, overcome by grace. Then he moved his mouth, teasing the corners of her lips with a whispering caress.

Her world went up in flames. The heat and desire were so unexpected, she nearly fell to her knees. As it was, she had to cling to him to stay upright. Every inch of her heated to boiling and her muscles trembled. Her breasts swelled against the suddenly unbearable confines of her bra. Her thighs quivered and refused to support her. Dear Lord, all this and he'd barely begun. How would she survive more?

She found out seconds later when his tongue touched her lips. Unable to do anything but react and feel, she parted to admit him. Lightning zapped through her, making her lean into him. She realized the hand that had been gently stroking her cheek now held her jaw in a firm grip. Not punishing, but she couldn't have escaped. Not that she wanted to. His other hand moved restlessly up and down her back, pausing at the curve of her derriere. When he squeezed her there, she arched toward him, her belly brushing against the hard ridge of his desire.

They caught their breath in unison. Then he plunged inside her mouth, tasting, tempting, pushing her into a passionate place that had no frame of reference, no reality save wanting. What her memory might have forgotten, her body remembered. She wanted him as she'd never wanted any man before.

She wrapped her arms around him. He was hard to her soft, all straining muscle and heat. His heart thundered in his chest, matching the rapid cadence of hers. The night air surrounded them in a cocoon of tropical magic. She prayed the kiss would never end.

But it did. Eventually he pulled back and the hold on her face lessened. He tilted her chin down and chastely kissed her forehead.

"I want you," he said. "I don't think this is smart, but there it is."

"I know."

She swallowed hard, wondering if he would blame her for what had just happened. Or would he assume she was easy and take her to his bed? There was no place she would rather be. But… It wasn't time. Not yet.

He did neither. Instead he led her back to the stone wall and urged her to sit down. Then he settled next to her and put his arm around her.

"Don't worry about the future," he told her. "If no one has come looking for you by Christmas, I'll find your family." He gave her a warm smile that belied the passion still smoldering in his dark gaze. "I promise."

"I believe you," she said. Only to find that she did.

Chapter Seven

"So she's still here," John said.

Jarrett shrugged and waited. His friend didn't make him wait long.

"Wasn't she supposed to return to the hotel the morning after we found her?" the doctor asked. "Weren't you the one so anxious to get rid of her that you wanted her moved that night?"

"Your point?"

"Oh, I don't have a point. I'm just enjoying watching you squirm."

"You're acting as if you caught me doing something wrong, John. The truth is, Ariel isn't here because of me. Anna Jane didn't want her to leave."

"Ariel?"

Jarrett turned in his desk chair until he faced the wide windows behind him. "Ariel. Our mystery guest. Again, my niece is responsible for her name. It's from a Disney movie about a mermaid.''

The morning had dawned perfectly clear, with bright skies and brighter water. Ariel and Anna Jane sat by the edge of the pool, with their backs to him. Both were dressed in swimsuits. He tried not to notice the curve of Ariel's hips or the slender line of her neck exposed because she wore her hair piled on her head.

"Hasn't anyone reported her missing?" John asked, coming up to stand beside Jarrett's chair.

"No. Not here or on the other islands."

"How strange. If I had a woman that beautiful in my life I wouldn't let her get away."

"No, you'd keep her around for a couple of weeks, then you'd let her go."

John chuckled. "You're hardly one to talk. At least I have relationships with women. You live like a monk."

"Are we back to that?" It was a familiar line of conversation.

"It's not healthy. I'm talking to you as your doctor. You need some female companionship. If nothing else, at least take the equipment for a test drive to see if it still works."

"It works," Jarrett said dryly.

What John didn't know, and what Jarrett wasn't likely to tell him, was that there had been women. Not many and not often, but sometimes when he took business trips, he found a lady to accompany him. He picked someone who understood his rule of no emotional entanglements. For those few days he allowed himself to experience the pleasures of physical intimacy. But only for a short period of time and never on the island.

Until last night. Until a stranger had touched him both physically and emotionally.

Without wanting to, he remembered kissing Ariel. She'd been soft and willing in his arms, giving as passionately as he. They'd created fire, and the heat had nearly overwhelmed him. Looking back, he wondered where he'd found the strength to turn away. All he'd wanted to do was pull her down onto the sand and make love with her. But he hadn't. Because he wasn't willing to risk caring, and until he was sure he could completely control his emotions, he was determined to keep his physical distance. Ariel got under his skin and that frightened the hell out of him.

Life would be a lot easier if he knew the truth about her.

If only he could prove her guilt or innocence. While he wanted to believe her story, a part of him held back.

"We're about to be invaded," John said.

Jarrett followed his gaze and saw that Anna Jane had spotted them. She waved, then headed for the back door. Seconds later her footsteps sounded in the foyer and she appeared in the office.

"Dr. John, Dr. John, did you come to see Ariel?" she asked, flinging herself at the man.

John bent and hugged her back. "No. I didn't know she was still here. But I'm glad she's doing well."

Anna Jane smiled. "She's all better, except for her memory. But I like that she can't remember. She's staying for Christmas."

He brushed her bangs from her face. "Aren't you lucky."

Anna Jane nodded vigorously. "We're going horseback riding this afternoon. Come with us, please."

"You know there's nothing I would like better, but I have to work this afternoon. It's my clinic afternoon for hotel employees."

"Okay. But you have to come with us next time."

He nodded solemnly. "I promise."

Jarrett watched his friend with the child. Even John found it easy to be with Anna Jane. Jarrett was learning, but it was slow. What was it Ariel had said Anna Jane needed from him? Love and stability. They sounded simple in theory, but in practice—he wasn't so sure he had it in him.

Anna Jane turned to look at him. "Are you still going away on business?" she asked.

"Yes. Sorry."

"But horses are more fun than business."

"You're very smart," John said, and winked. "But I'm not sure your uncle Jarrett would agree. He loves business and I suspects he only tolerates horses."

Anna Jane's eyes widened. "Don't you like horses, Uncle Jarrett?"

He glared at his friend. "I like them fine. If I didn't already have a commitment, I would be happy to come with you. Even though I was your second choice."

She frowned for a second, then her face brightened. "You mean because I asked Dr. John first?"

John grinned. "Can I help it if the ladies prefer me?"

Anna Jane walked over and stood in front of Jarrett. Her small fingers caught at him. "Dr. John is very nice," she said, her tone serious. "But you're my uncle Jarrett and I love you very much."

Jarrett felt as if he'd been sucker punched. He squatted down in front of the child and cupped her cheek. He wanted to tell her he loved her, too, but he'd never said the words in his life. He wasn't sure he knew how. "Thank you," he said. "I feel very special. Now, go have a good time and I'll see you tomorrow."

Anna Jane gave him a quick kiss on the cheek and

scurried from the room. "I'll tell Ariel you said goodbye to her, too," she called as she left.

He watched her go. His life had been turned upside down by the arrival of one little girl. When combined with his mystery guest, he wondered if he would ever be the same. He turned to the window and watched as Anna Jane skipped into view. She had an animated conversation with Ariel and they both laughed.

God knows he wanted to be able to trust the woman. He was nearly willing to believe in her. But— Always a "but" to hold him back. He wanted to be sure.

John said something, but Jarrett wasn't listening. A plan appeared fully formed, a brilliant idea that would help him know if Ariel was really who she appeared to be or simply a fabulous actress hoping to get lucky.

Ariel pulled on a pair of jeans and fastened them. The fit wasn't perfect, but they would do for an afternoon on horseback. It wasn't as if she had to make a fashion statement. She was looking forward to her outing. Not only would she be able to explore the island and see if anything sparked her memory, she would find out if she knew how to ride. When she'd said she wasn't sure whether she'd ever been on a horse, Anna Jane had promised a very gentle mount. Ariel hoped the girl knew what she was talking about.

When someone knocked on her door, she called, "Come in."

But instead of Anna Jane or Leona, Jarrett walked into her room. Her breath caught in her throat and her chest tightened.

He was stunning.

Instead of his usual trousers and polo shirt, or even jeans, he wore a gray suit, complete with a crisp white shirt and silk tie. He'd recently showered and shaved, and he looked as if he'd stepped from the pages of a men's magazine.

She wanted to touch his face and feel his smooth, warm skin. She wanted to inhale the scent of him, to be held by him and know his strength again. Although she'd done her best to forget the kiss they'd shared the previous night, she hadn't been able to. Now, seeing him again brought it all back. Her body ached with the passion he'd aroused in her. Fire raced up her thighs, while flames heated her breasts.

She wanted him, which was understandable under the circumstances. He'd kissed her in a way that had left her shaken and hungry with needs she had forgotten existed. But what was more frightening was that she was finally ready to admit she liked him. Last night, when she'd been vulnerable and hurting, he'd held her close and comforted her. Despite his concerns that she was faking her memory loss and was potentially a horrible person, he was kind and gentle. And she admired how he was trying to make a home for his niece.

Liking and wanting were a deadly combination. Even without the benefit of her memory and past experiences, she knew she was in trouble. Jarrett held himself apart from the world. She didn't know what his secrets were, but sensed they were as much a part of him as the color of his eyes. He would never be what she needed a man to be. Yet that didn't stop her heart from thundering as he leaned one shoulder against the door frame and gave her a lazy smile.

"How committed are you to this horseback-riding trip?" he asked.

The low, sultry tones of his voice slipped down her spine like liquid satin. Her mind didn't understand what he was asking, but her body didn't care. "I, um, want to go."

"Too bad. My business to St. Thomas is going to keep me there overnight. I thought you might care to join me. I would be busy this afternoon, but we could have dinner together tonight."

Alone. He didn't say the word—he didn't have to. She heard it loud and clear. A night alone with Jarrett. She tried to swallow but couldn't. Her gaze met his and she read the passion there. Passion and something else. Something dark. Then he blinked and only the desire remained.

Alone with Jarrett on a tropical island paradise. Just the two of them and the night. Every cell in her body rippled in anticipation. How could she refuse? How could she risk saying yes? Things would happen if they went away together. Things that she wasn't ready to deal with. Besides, she'd made a promise to Anna Jane.

"I can't," she said regretfully. "I would like to, but it's just not going to work out."

One dark eyebrow rose slightly. "You're not tempted?"

"More than you know," she blurted out.

"Then what's the problem? If nothing else, the free afternoon would give you time to explore the city. You might recognize something."

She hadn't thought of that. "I would like to, but I'll have to pass. I told Anna Jane that we'd go horseback riding and I don't want to disappoint her."

His posture didn't shift, but she could have sworn his body tightened. "She'll get over it."

She shook her head. "I gave her my word. Besides, I don't want to leave her alone."

"Leona and Frank will be here."

There was something else going on, something she didn't understand. Ariel was sure of it. "Right now Anna Jane needs to be with people who keep their promises. She's been abandoned enough for one lifetime. I'm not going to do anything that might hurt her."

Jarrett stared at her for a long time. Then he took a step closer, leaned toward her and kissed her cheek. "Thank you," he murmured, and was gone.

More confused than ever, Ariel stared after him. What had that been about? Why was he thanking her? She shrugged and resolved to put him out of her mind. At least until he'd returned from his trip.

Jarrett fastened his seat belt and nodded at the pilot. Instantly the jet engines roared as the small plane rolled forward down the runway. The flight would take less than twenty minutes, barely enough time for him to glance at a magazine. But instead of reading, he turned toward the window. As they rose gently into the sky and banked northeast, he caught a glimpse of the beach by his house. He wondered if Ariel and his niece had already left for their horseback-riding trip.

If Ariel's plan had been to seduce him, he'd given her the perfect opportunity. But she hadn't taken the bait. Instead she'd kept her promise to a nine-year-old child, insisting that was more important than a night of passion. If he hadn't felt her trembling response the previous evening, he might have been insulted. But he knew Ariel had wanted him as much as he'd wanted her.

So now he could make his decision about trusting her. He was finally willing to believe she was who she claimed—a woman with no memory of her past. He should be pleased. And he was. Except for the fact that what had started out as a simple test had instead become a genuine request. He wanted Ariel to be with him now. He wanted to have her join him for dinner and to spend the night with her. He wanted to be with her and he wanted to make love to her.

Which made the guilt difficult to ignore. He'd been wrong to mention the possibility of her recognizing something on the island. Now that he believed her story, his taunt had been cruel and unnecessary.

The view changed to vivid blue sea. He straightened in his leather seat and closed his eyes. He would make it up to her, he decided. For as long as she wanted to stay, he would give her a place in which to recover from her memory loss. She would spend Christmas with Anna Jane and himself so she wouldn't have to be by herself. She would be a part of the family. A temporary member so she wouldn't feel so alone.

Anna Jane glanced around the dining room. "I miss Uncle Jarrett," she said.

"Me, too," Ariel agreed, then realized she was telling the truth. She *did* miss Jarrett. While he didn't always talk a lot at the table, his presence had power and even in silence he dominated the room. Tonight, despite the lights overhead, the room felt dark and empty. As if the heart of it was gone.

You are in more trouble than you know, Ariel told herself. Lord help her, she was falling for him. It was an intolerable situation. She refused to be attracted to a man who wouldn't let himself trust her. But did she have a choice in the matter? Was it too late for her to turn back? Unfortunately, she didn't have an answer to that one.

"Is he coming back tomorrow?" Anna Jane asked.

"That's what he said. Did he come talk to you and explain about the trip?"

Anna Jane nodded. "He said he would just be gone overnight, but I wanted to check for sure. Sometimes grown-ups go away and never come back."

Ariel stretched her hand across the table and squeezed the girl's fingers. "Uncle Jarrett isn't like most people," she said. "He cares about you. Don't worry, he'll be back." Too late she remembered that the people in Anna Jane's life hadn't left because they'd wanted to. Her nanny had been unable to return because of an ill family member and her mother had gone away by dying.

But the child seemed to accept the explanation. She finished the last couple of bites of her rice, then pushed her empty plate away. "I have to get Uncle Jarrett something for Christmas. Leona said to look through some catalogs and order it, but is it too late for that?"

"With overnight mail, anything is possible. Do you have anything special in mind?"

Anna Jane scrunched up her nose. "I want to get him a nice pen. The one he uses at his desk is all scratched. Plus, they can put writing on it and then he'd always know it's his."

"What a great idea."

Anna Jane chatted on about another couple of ideas. As Ariel listened, she realized she'd grown accustomed to spending time with the little girl and would miss her terribly when she had to leave. Somehow, in a very few days, she'd made a life for herself on St. Alicia. But it wasn't the real world. Her life—wherever and whatever that was—waited for her. It was just a matter of time until she began remembering more or something triggered her memory to return.

She wondered what she would find when she remembered. Had this experience changed her? Would she like that other person, the real woman who lived in this body?

When she returned to herself would she still feel the same about Jarrett, or would her emotions be tempered by different life experiences?

What would happen if she didn't remember? Where would she go? How did one go about finding a lost life, and if she had nowhere else to be, however would she find it in herself to leave Jarrett?

Chapter Eight

Anna Jane leaned back against the tree base and stared up at the sky. If she squinted hard, she thought she could make out the tiny dot that was her uncle's plane. But in a couple of seconds she realized it was just a bird. She giggled, wondering what Uncle Jarrett would think if she told him she thought he was a bird. He would probably smile. He might even laugh. Ever since Ariel had arrived, her uncle had been smiling and laughing more. That made her happy.

She looked around at all the brush and trees. The island was very beautiful. Sometimes she missed New York. All the people and the noises and the smells. But most of the time she liked the island better. She could think here. Sometimes she thought about Nana B. and how much she missed her. Her chest hurt then, and she wanted to cry. When she gave in to the tears, she felt sad, but relieved. Here on the island it was easier to cry. In the city she'd worried about doing the right thing a lot.

A hum caught her attention. She glanced up and saw a tiny, glinting object in the sky. It moved toward her, growing larger and larger. She stood and began to wave. She didn't know if Uncle Jarrett could see her yet, but she knew he was looking for her. She knew when he saw her he would wave back.

She knew he loved her. Oh, he couldn't say the words, but when she told him she loved him, his face got all tight and he swallowed. She'd seen him. When she'd first arrived, she hadn't been sure he wanted her here. She knew he wasn't used to children. Her mother had told her that many times when she'd explained why Uncle Jarrett had never come to visit. But he was getting used to having her around.

Just as he was getting used to having Ariel around. Anna Jane clasped her hands together to hold in her excitement. When she thought about the two of them, she was happy inside. They looked at each other differently than they looked at other people.

"Oh, please, Lord, let Ariel and my uncle fall in love," she whispered, praying as she did several times each day. She hoped God was listening. She didn't care about getting presents for Christmas...well, maybe she cared a little, but more than anything she wanted her uncle and Ariel to be together. She liked having Ariel around. She made Uncle Jarrett laugh. She made Anna Jane feel better about missing Nana B. Ariel was the best part of her mother and Nana B. all in one. She could be happy on this island with her uncle and Ariel. They could all be happy.

The plane swooped down out of the sky. She waved harder and at last could see her uncle in the window waving back. She grinned and ran toward the edge of the runway.

Ariel paced restlessly in the library. The quiet of the house was oppressive. Although she loved the place and thought it was stunningly beautiful, with Jarrett away it was just an empty house.

The worst of it was he'd been gone less than twenty-four hours. If she was moping this much now, what would it be like when she had to leave? How would she survive missing him?

As she scanned the titles of books in his library, hoping to find something to read, her mind wandered. She thought about the possibility of staying. She could be happy here—with Jarrett. At least, that's what her body had told her last night when she couldn't sleep. The restlessness had sent her pacing back and forth in her bedroom until nearly dawn. She'd thought about Jarrett's invitation and had wondered what it had meant. She hadn't regretted spending time with Anna Jane. She'd enjoyed both their afternoon riding and their quiet evening together. But a part of her had longed to be with Jarrett.

She strolled around the library, picking up a book only to flip through the pages, then put it back. Nothing caught her eye. Nothing could distract her from the physical need to see him again. Maybe she should have gone with Anna Jane to wait for the plane. She shook her head. It would be more special for the little girl to meet her uncle and have private time with him. The two of them needed to keep bonding. They needed to form a family unit.

Wouldn't it be nice if she were a part of that? Could she really be happy here, on the island? Ariel knew there was no way to answer that question until she knew who she was. All her feelings for Jarrett were based on the fact that she didn't have a past.

She pushed another book back onto the shelf and glanced at the clock, wishing time would move more quickly. She wanted Jarrett home. She wanted to see him and hear his voice. She wanted his gaze to settle on her so her breath would quicken and her chest get tight. She wanted to kiss him and—

Her foot bumped into something and she stumbled. As she caught her balance, she noticed a box sticking out from the bottom shelf, and she bent to look at it. The gray cardboard box was one of those containers designed to hold magazines. She pulled it out and flipped through the contents.

The eclectic collection made no sense. Most of them were business magazines, but not different issues of the same one. There were a few small newspapers tucked in, as well. Ariel sat on the floor and pulled out the first magazine. She leafed through it, wondering why Jarrett had kept it. Then she turned the page and she knew. There was an article about him.

She checked them all, and that was what the publications had in common. Each had featured Jarrett or his company in some way. She returned to the first one and started to read.

He'd given her a thumbnail sketch of his past, so she wasn't surprised as the journalist outlined Jarrett's brilliant rescue of the family's failing hotel business. She'd known he'd completed college in just three years, but she hadn't guessed it had been Harvard. In fact, she hadn't actually grasped the fact that Jarrett owned a hotel chain. The man was wealthy, successful and powerful. Why hadn't she noticed?

Ariel bit her lower lip to hold in a faint moan. Dear

God, she'd been living in the home of a reclusive millionaire and she hadn't given it a moment's thought. He wasn't just a guy who had been nice enough to offer her a place to stay. He made deals worth billions; he had an empire. No wonder he hadn't trusted her.

She continued to read the articles. Most of them went over the same material. A few featured acquisitions and two were about the building of the jewel in the crown of the Wilkenson chain—the resort on St. Alicia. He'd accomplished so much in such a short period of time. He was brilliant and gifted and resourceful and she didn't need her memory back to know she was definitely out of her league.

She turned a page in the magazine and saw a shaded sidebar. The title of it was Romantic Mystery Haunts Tycoon's Past. Ariel stiffened, then forced herself to relax as she read. There wasn't much information, just a brief story about how there were rumors of a romantic entanglement in Jarrett's past. No details were mentioned, just hints that an explosive love had gone desperately wrong. A woman had mysteriously died in a fire in Jarrett's home. He hadn't been there at the time, nor had he made any comment about the woman or the fire that had reduced the structure to ashes. Shortly after the fire, the resort on St. Alicia had been completed and Jarrett had taken up residence on the island. He'd been a recluse ever since.

Ariel closed the magazine and hugged it to her chest. Who was the woman and why hadn't she been able to escape the fire? What was the secret of Jarrett's past? She realized with dismay that she was upset by the news that he'd been involved with someone. That another woman had touched his heart and his soul. Even as she told herself she was being crazy, she knew all the words in the world wouldn't matter. Her feelings for Jarrett were a tangled mess that showed no signs of getting straightened out.

But it didn't matter. The magazine articles had confirmed what she'd already sensed. She might not remember her past or know who she was, but she didn't belong in his world, either.

Anna Jane rolled the dice. When she quickly counted up the squares, she yelped with excitement. "Another railroad. I want to buy it."

Ariel raised her eyebrows. "She's a real estate tycoon. It must be in the genes."

Jarrett pointed to her properties, dotted with green houses and red hotels. "You're not doing too badly yourself. Although I'd like to talk you out of a couple of addresses."

"Not a chance." She grinned and tossed her head. Blond curls went flying.

He chuckled. They'd been playing for the past couple of hours. There were several faxes and E-mail messages waiting for him, but he couldn't bring himself to leave the living room to take care of business. Maybe for the first time in his life something else was more important.

He glanced around the room. Despite the fact that it was still afternoon and plenty warm, a fire glowed brightly in the fireplace. Anna Jane had mentioned how nice it would be. Real log fires were a part of her holiday celebration and he hadn't wanted to disappoint her. The large Christmas tree twinkled in the corner. There were boughs of pine all around the room and decorations on tables, walls and over door frames. He tried to remember the last time he'd been in a home that had been decorated for the holidays, and couldn't. He was grateful to Ariel for suggesting he do this. Not only for Anna Jane, who deserved some care in her life, but also for himself. He needed a little cheer, too.

Ariel rolled the dice and rounded the board, collecting her money with a triumphant wave. "Time for more real estate. I'm having trouble keeping up with you tycoon types."

Anna Jane laughed. The high, pure sound caused his heart to ache with emotion. Maybe Tracy hadn't been wrong to name him guardian of her daughter. He still wasn't sure of his way, but he'd come to care for the child more than he'd thought possible.

A voice in the back of his mind mocked him. Was he thinking of a family at this late date in his life? He silenced the voice with the reminder that he was thirty-two. Hardly an old man. A family was a real possibility. Except for one thing—he knew the danger of getting involved. No one had to teach him that lesson twice. Early on he'd resolved never to love anyone, and his past had only reinforced that decision. He wasn't going to change his mind now. Caring about Anna Jane was safe because she was a relative and a child. He would be a second father to her—that he could handle. Loving a woman was something else entirely. Love and trust weren't in his vocabulary.

And yet... He watched Ariel absently brush her hair off her shoulders. Her shorts and T-shirt weren't stylish or expensive, yet they enticed him more than any seductive gown could have. She sat cross-legged, her honey-colored thighs within touching distance. His fingers itched to feel her smooth skin. He wanted to hold her and kiss her and—

"Uncle Jarrett, it's your turn," Anna Jane announced, holding out the dice. "You're not paying attention."

"Sorry."

He rolled and landed on one of Ariel's hotels, then winced when she announced the rent. "I could give you a break," she said. "After all, you've been a gracious host."

He gazed into her green eyes. "Maybe we could work out a trade."

It took a couple of seconds for his suggestion to sink in, then her mouth parted in surprise as color climbed up her cheeks to her hairline.

"You have to pay, Uncle Jarrett," Anna Jane said. "You can't weasel out of it."

He raised his eyebrows. "Are you calling me a weasel?"

The girl smiled. "No. But you're acting like one."

He pounced on her, pulling her close and tickling her. She squealed. "Let me go, let me go," she gasped between giggles.

She pushed at his chest.

With a last tickle along her ribs, he released her. Instead of moving away, the girl snuggled close and rested her head on his chest. "We missed you while you were gone."

He touched Anna Jane's smooth hair. "I missed you, too."

She glanced up at him. "Both of us?"

His gaze flicked to Ariel, who was watching them. "Both of you."

His words were for the child, but the meaning belonged to the woman. He *had* missed her. More than he should have...more than he'd wanted to. Usually he lost himself in business, but not yesterday or this morning. Again and again his attention had strayed as he'd thought about what Anna Jane and Ariel were up to on the island.

He'd wanted to be with them, watching them, laughing with them.

A knock on the open door made them all look up. Leona put her hands on her hips. "I don't want to interrupt the game, but you, little one, insisted you were going to help me with my next batch of cookies. I'm going to start them now. You can help or you can continue to play your game. It's up to you."

Anna Jane scrambled to her feet. "I'll help with the cookies," she said as she dashed to the door. Then she glanced back at him. "Is that all right, Uncle Jarrett? Can we finish the game later?"

"No problem."

"Thanks." She ran ahead of Leona and clattered toward the kitchen.

Ariel moved the board game across the floor until it was under the coffee table, then leaned back against the sofa. She stretched her long legs out on the hardwood floor. "She has so much energy. Sometimes I get tired just watching her."

"She is amazing."

Ariel looked at him. "You seem to be more comfortable with her."

"I am." He shrugged. "Like you said, it's not that hard. I try to pay attention to her and care about her. She's a great kid."

"You're a pretty great uncle. She adores you."

"Now," he agreed. "Wait until she's a teenager and I won't let her borrow the car. Then she'll hate me."

"True." Ariel grinned. "I would love to see what you're going to put the boys through before you let them take her out on a date."

Dating? He hadn't thought that far ahead. "I don't think I can handle it. She won't be allowed to date."

"Oh, there's a realistic solution, Jarrett. Lock her up in a tower. Think of how balanced her personality will be. Very clever."

He leaned forward and touched her nose with the tip of his finger. "You have a sarcastic streak, don't you?"

"No. Why would you say that?" Her smile belied her words. Then the smile faded and she searched his face as if trying to figure something out.

"What?" he asked.

"I—" She broke off and ducked her head. "I have a confession."

His gut clenched. He didn't want to hear any confessions. Not now. Not when he'd just started believing in her. He should have known better than to trust her. Dammit, when was he going to learn? He braced himself and nodded. "Go on."

"I, um, was in the library today."

"That's hardly a hanging offense," he said lightly, wishing the sick feeling would go away.

"Yes, well, I found some things I probably shouldn't have." She picked at the hem of her shorts and shrugged. "I was looking for a book to read and I couldn't find one. Then I kicked this box." She raised her head. Her eyes had darkened to the color of emeralds. "I saw the magazine articles and I read them."

He waited. She stared at him. Silence.

"That's it?" he asked, nearly too stunned to be relieved. "You read the magazine articles?"

"Yes."

"If I was worried about keeping them a secret, I would have locked them away."

"Are you sure?"

"They were printed nationally, Ariel. You could have looked them up in the local library."

She smiled faintly. "I suspect there isn't a library on St. Alicia. I don't want you to think I was prying. I wasn't. Well, maybe a little. It's just that when I realized what they all had in common, I couldn't help reading."

Relief flooded him like cool, clear water after a desert hike. The pain in his chest eased, as did his breathing. Confessions like this he could handle.

"What did you think?" he asked.

She pulled her knees to her chest and wrapped her arms around her legs. "You're someone important, but I'd sort of guessed that one."

"Hardly important."

"You turned the family business around in a big way and very quickly. It's impressive."

He was pleased. He wanted her to be impressed. Then his pleasure faded. He remembered something else from the articles—they'd hinted at the dark secret in his past. No doubt Ariel had read about that, too. She would have questions.

He leaned back against the sofa and rubbed the bridge of his nose. One day he was going to find a way to leave the past behind.

"I think I understand now," she said softly. "Of course you couldn't trust me. A man in your position has to worry about security and strangers. I'm sorry I was such a bother."

"You weren't a bother. A slightly unexpected guest, but is that so bad?"

"I guess not. You've been great," she declared earnestly. "I really appreciate it. You've given me a place to stay while I try to sort things out. I just wish I could remember."

For the first time since her arrival, he wasn't looking

forward to that moment. He didn't want her to remember, because he didn't want her to go. At least, not yet.

"I've said I'll help you, and I will," he said. "Let's get through the holidays first, then worry about your memory. Besides, it might have already returned by then."

"Wouldn't that be nice? Or maybe someone will come looking for me."

Jarrett didn't respond. While he didn't want Ariel to be alone in the world, he wasn't looking forward to her being reunited with anyone—especially if that someone was a man.

He realized she hadn't said anything about the fire or the woman who had died. She must have read about it in the magazines. Was she waiting for him to bring it up? He might. In time. As a rule he didn't talk about the past, but Ariel was someone who could understand.

"There's a call," Leona said, poking her head into the room. "Jarrett, it's your manager from the hotel."

"I'll take it in the office," he replied as he rose to his feet. He glanced at Ariel. "Be right back."

She smiled. "I'll be waiting."

The slow curve of her lips hit him below the belt. Need rose instantly. How long did it take to mix up cookies, and would he have time to steal a kiss or two when he returned?

He crossed the foyer and entered his office, then punched the blinking red light and picked up the phone.

"Mr. Wilkenson, you'll be so pleased," the manager said. "The mystery has been solved. There are two couples standing right here in my office looking for your houseguest."

At first Jarrett didn't understand what he was hearing.

Then he did. He sank onto his chair and closed his eyes. He couldn't think, couldn't breathe, could only listen.

"The two ladies say she's their sister. She came in a few days early. The reservation was for everyone. That's why we couldn't find a match for a single woman."

He hadn't known how much it was going to hurt to lose her until she was gone. He clutched the phone more tightly. "What is her name?"

He heard the manager repeat the question. "Fallon Bedford. She's a schoolteacher from San Francisco."

"Are you sure these people are really her family?"

The manager laughed. "Yes, sir. They're her sisters. No doubt about that. What? Just a minute."

There was muffled conversation, then a feminine voice spoke into the phone. "Mr. Wilkenson, my name is Elissa Stephenson. I understand my sister is with you?"

The voices were similar. It was true, then. She'd been found.

"Yes, she's here and she's fine."

"Your manager explained about the accident."

"She's very healthy, Mrs. Stephenson. I had my personal physician take care of her. The only problem seems to be with her memory."

There was more muffled conversation. The ache filled him, startling him with its intensity.

"I can't believe this," Elissa said. "We have to see her."

"Of course. Tell my manager to bring you right over. The trip is only a few minutes."

"We'll be there." She paused. "Are you going to tell her? I don't want this to be too much of a shock."

"Sure. I'll let her know. See you shortly."

He hung up and sat there staring at nothing. The inevitable had occurred. He'd known this was going to happen—he'd even wanted it to happen. Until it had.

He hadn't even thought to ask if she was married. The manager had said two couples. Did he dare hope? Then he reminded himself it didn't matter. Better if she was married. She would leave, and his life could return to normal. He didn't have time for all this foolishness.

But the words that had always worked in the past had somehow lost their magic. Instead of relieved, he felt hollow and defeated. Then he groaned softly. If he felt this way, how was Anna Jane going to deal with the situation?

He walked into the living room. Anna Jane had returned. She took one look at his face and stood. Her small hands clutched at each other. Her face paled and he saw a tremor ripple through her.

"Uncle Jarrett?"

The tone of her voice alerted Ariel...make that Fallon. Their mysterious stranger glanced at him and jumped. "What happened? Did you get bad news?"

"Not at all," he said, and tried to make his expression pleasant. "Actually, it's good news."

He crossed to his niece and touched her on the shoulder. "It's okay. Everyone is fine."

The child relaxed visibly. "I got scared."

"I know. I'm sorry. I didn't mean to frighten you."

Ariel—he gave himself a mental shake—Fallon stood. "Jarrett? You're terrifying us. What's going on?"

"Your family has been found. They arrived on the island a few hours ago and have been looking for you. Apparently you have two sisters who are married. The reservation was for the five of you, which is why we couldn't find it."

He watched her closely, waiting to see if she remembered anything. She frowned, then shook her head. "The news isn't triggering anything. Sisters? Two of them?"

"I spoke to one named Elissa."

She repeated the name. "Did they say who I was?"

Small hands took hold of his. He moved closer to Anna Jane and squeezed back. Tears filled her dark eyes, but they didn't fall. He knew they would—tonight—when she was alone.

"You're Fallon Bedford. A schoolteacher from San Francisco."

"This is so strange. I can't even take this in or believe it. I don't know what to think. Are they coming over, or do you want me to go there?"

"They're on their way. They should be here any minute."

Confusion clouded her eyes and twisted her mouth. "Family," she murmured. "I can't believe it. I do belong somewhere." She gave him a tentative smile. "If only I could remember where that was."

There was a knock at the front door. He took a step toward the foyer. Anna Jane released him and retreated to the safety of the sofa. He knew about her pain. They would have to talk about it later.

He crossed to the door and pulled it open. He wasn't sure what he'd expected. Maybe someone who looked a little like Fallon. A stranger with a hint of her around eyes or smile. Instead two identical replicas of Fallon stood there. One wore shorts and a T-shirt, the other a long gauzy sundress. But those were the only differences. From the color of their hair, to the worried expressions, to their bodies, they were exactly like her.

The woman in the dress said, "I'm Elissa, Mr. Wilkenson. We spoke a minute ago. Is my sister here?"

"Yes. Please come in."

He heard footsteps behind him. Fallon approached. When she saw her sisters, she paused. She swayed as if she might lose her balance. Jarrett was at her side in an instant, and he put an arm around her to steady her. Her eyes fluttered closed, then opened. She blinked twice and he knew. In less than a heartbeat her memory had been restored.

Chapter Nine

Everyone was talking at once. Fallon smiled as her sisters and their husbands explained once again how stunned they'd been when they'd been unable to find her at the resort.

"It was as if you'd disappeared off the face of the planet," Kayla said.

"In a way, I suppose I had," Fallon told her, still feeling a little shaky.

Her memory had returned in a flash. For a second the world had gone dark, then suddenly she'd been fine. The sensation was odd. The closest she could come to explaining it was having her ears plug on a flight. There was that feeling of talking through a tunnel and not being able to hear very well. When her eardrums popped, everything was normal again.

That's how she felt now. Restored. Although it was

odd to have herself back and yet remember not remembering.

She glanced around the room and saw Anna Jane sitting alone on the sofa. The girl looked as stunned as she felt. No doubt the sight of ''Ariel's'' sisters was a little unnerving for the child.

Fallon crossed to her and took a seat. "How are you doing?" she asked.

Anna Jane shrugged. "Okay. I'm glad you got your memory back and you have a family."

The words were polite and exactly what she should have said, but Fallon saw the truth in the pain in her eyes. She hugged the child close. "I know this makes things different, but just because I remembered my past doesn't mean I've forgotten about you. You're still very special to me."

"Really?" Her lower lip trembled. "I wondered if you would forget."

"I could never forget you." She smoothed Anna Jane's bangs out of her eyes. "Didn't we just go horseback riding yesterday and order presents for your uncle? I haven't forgotten anything."

"Good." Anna Jane snuggled close. "You're my best friend." She giggled. "It's gonna be weird calling you Fallon."

"I'll tell you a little secret." Fallon leaned close and whispered in her ear. "All my sisters and I hate our names. They're strange. Kids made fun of us when we were growing up. We always wanted normal, pretty names, like yours."

"Anna Jane isn't pretty."

"You're right," Fallon said earnestly. "It's beautiful."

Anna Jane flushed with pleasure, then turned to the sisters. "Are you really triplets?"

Elissa heard the question. "We sure are," she said, oving closer and crouching in front of the child. "Identical from birth. Of course, that's just on the outside. We're different on the inside."

"I'd like to hear about that," Jarrett said, stepping into the room. He carried a tray with drinks. Behind him, Leona had plates of cookies.

"I helped with some of the cookies," Anna Jane said.

Elissa sat on the other side of the girl. "Tell me which ones. I want to taste those."

Cole walked to the sofa and perched on the arm by his wife. Kayla and Patrick settled on the love seat opposite. Jarrett passed out drinks to everyone.

Kayla leaned forward. As usual, she wore her hair in a ponytail. Her face was devoid of makeup, yet she looked radiant.

"How are you feeling?" Fallon asked, remembering that her sister was three months pregnant.

"Fabulous, but I don't want to talk about that. What happened? How did you lose your memory?"

"I don't remember," Fallon teased.

Kayla rolled her eyes. "I see you're still as difficult as ever."

"I'm not difficult."

"You can be," Elissa said. "But not this time. Tell us what you do remember."

"I found a note in a bottle," she said.

"I wrote it." Anna Jane straightened. Her smile faded. "I didn't mean for you to get hurt, though."

"I know, honey. It all worked out." Fallon squeezed her hand. "The note was from Anna Jane and she was looking for a friend. On the back was a map of the island.

I spoke to one of the bartenders and he told me about Jarrett's house here, but he didn't know anything about a little girl. He's the one who told me I could walk on the beach all the way up. It seemed like a good idea at the time."

Jarrett handed her a glass of soda. "We talked to all the staff. No one said they'd talked to you."

"I know. Joshua was leaving that afternoon to go home for the holidays. He wasn't around to be interviewed."

"I should have thought of that," Jarrett said as he put the now-empty tray on the table and sat in the wing chair by the tree.

"You'll know for next time," she teased.

He raised his eyebrows at her. They shared a quick look that was as much a connection as any conversation or touch. For that split second she knew what he was thinking. The pure moment left her breathless. One question had been answered in spades. Getting her memory back hadn't changed her feelings about Jarrett at all. She still admired him, liked him and wanted him. The only difference was, now she knew for certain there wasn't another man in her life.

"Did you fall and hit your head?" Elissa asked.

"No. I fell asleep on a beach in a cove, when I stopped for lunch." She wrinkled her nose. "Unfortunately it was underwater at high tide. I woke up floating. When I tried to swim around the rocks, I was caught up in the waves and hit my head on the cliffs. That's the last I remember."

"I found her," Anna Jane said, picking up the story. "She was washed up on the beach. Then Uncle Jarrett called the doctor and they brought her inside. She woke up and didn't remember who she was."

Neither Kayla nor Elissa looked relieved by the telling of the story. "How badly were you hurt?" Kayla asked, clutching Patrick's hand.

"Just a few bruises." Fallon touched her face. "They're gone now. Except for the memory loss, I was fine in a couple of days. Jarrett was nice enough to let me stay here."

She glanced at him again. He gave her a quick smile. Instantly her heartbeat increased and she felt her skin get all prickly.

Jarrett picked up the story. "I made inquiries at the hotel, but no one came forward to claim her. When we checked reservations, there weren't any for a single person."

He outlined the events of the past week. Fallon noticed he never mentioned his distrust of her, which wasn't surprising. She wondered what he thought of her now. Obviously she *had* lost her memory and wasn't the gold digger he'd feared. Would that change things between them? She decided it wouldn't. In the past couple of days Jarrett seemed to have made a decision about her. His willingness to talk about his past proved that. Obviously he'd decided to believe her even before he'd found out the truth. The realization made her glow from the inside out.

As Jarrett continued to talk with her sisters and their husbands, Fallon rose to her feet and crossed to the window. She turned around and studied the room. The homey scene made her feel content. Her sisters were here, and she was with Jarrett and Anna Jane. It was as if she'd finally found a place to belong.

She stifled a smile. Obviously, she was taking too much for granted in the situation. She'd been a houseguest forced on Jarrett. He'd come to accept her, but that didn't mean he thought of her as special. Except that he'd kissed and held her. Had that meant as much to him as it had to her?

Now, with her memory back, she knew that while men had kissed her in the past, none of them had moved her the same way. She'd never found herself clinging to a man, wanting to touch and be touched.

She brushed her hands over her shorts. At the smooth feel of the fabric, she glanced down. The casual white shorts and cropped peach T-shirt weren't anything like her normal tailored style. She fingered her loose hair. That was different, too. Yet she still felt comfortable. Had being Ariel changed Fallon? Had losing her memory allowed her to develop a different side of her personality?

"But why did you come here without your sisters?" Anna Jane asked, drawing Fallon back into the conversation.

She shrugged. "Some of it was just circumstances. The school year ended a little early and I thought it would be fun to spend some time in paradise on my own." She shook her head. "I was wrong. Within twenty-four hours I was tired of my own company. That's why I was so excited when I found your note in the bottle. It was a mystery and it gave me something to do."

"What if you hadn't come early?" Anna Jane asked. "You wouldn't have found my note and then you wouldn't be here now."

Without conscious thought, Fallon glanced at Jarrett. He met her gaze. What if, she thought. What if Anna Jane was right? Then she, Fallon, never would have met the precious child or her tempting uncle. Was that all this was—a quirk of fate?

"Weren't you terrified?" Elissa asked. "I can't imagine what it would be like not to remember who I was."

"The worst was that I thought no one was looking for me," Fallon told her. "I couldn't believe I was alone."

"At least now I know why you never called," Kayla said. "I kept expecting you to phone with an update on how you liked the resort." She covered her mouth for a second and grinned. "Not that it isn't fabulous, Jarrett."

"Thanks." He leaned forward in his chair. "Now it's my turn to ask a few questions, if you don't mind."

"Sure," Elissa and Kayla said together. Fallon didn't say anything. She wasn't so sure.

She knew she was right to worry when she saw the twinkle in Jarrett's dark eyes. "Obviously the three of you are identical triplets, but one of you mentioned being different on the inside." He glanced between her two sisters before settling on Kayla. "You said Fallon was difficult. How?"

Fallon was impressed that he could already tell the triplets apart. She knew there were enough minor differences that close friends and family knew who was whom, and their different styles of dressing helped. Even so, strangers found the task impossible. She supposed Jarrett would be able to pick her out easily, which left deciding between Kayla and Elissa. Still, he'd done well.

Kayla laughed. "Gee, big sister, should I spill all your secrets?"

"No," Fallon said. "But you're not going to listen to me anyway. You never do."

"True," Kayla agreed brightly. "Okay, here goes. Fallon is the oldest, Elissa is in the middle, and I'm the youngest. Because she had those first few minutes as an only child, Fallon is the boss of everything. When we were growing up, she used to tell us what to do all the time."

Fallon leaned against the window frame. "That is so

untrue. I tried to be responsible while you were running around like a maniac.''

"Right." Kayla dismissed her with a wave and turned toward Jarrett. "She's very conservative and proper. You know, the cliché of a schoolteacher. Fallon always does the right thing. She makes these lists about everything and organizes her life. And she expects the same from the rest of us. This makes her difficult.''

"I do not expect the same from you, and this is not flattering," Fallon said, not sure she wanted Jarrett to have all this information about her. Her sister spoke the truth, yet it was so different from how she'd felt while she'd been Ariel.

"I'm getting to the good part. Fallon is also very caring and would do anything for any of us." Kayla's humor faded. "We love her and don't want anything to happen to her. So we're very grateful to you for rescuing her.''

"I'm glad I could help," Jarrett said.

"There were twins at my school," Anna Jane said. "They used to dress alike.''

"We did, too," Elissa said. "I liked it.''

Kayla made a gagging noise. "It was awful.''

"I'm going to have to side with the baby on this one," Fallon told Elissa. "I hated dressing alike. Do you remember those awful dresses Mom made us wear for personal appearances?'' She grimaced at the memory. "Pink and white checks, with a white collar and puffy sleeves. I felt like a dress-up doll.''

"They were pretty," Elissa protested.

"Oh, please." Kayla rolled her eyes.

Jarrett glanced at Fallon. "Personal appearances?''

The triplets glanced at each other in silent communication. "That one just slipped out," Fallon said. "Oh, well. There's no point in trying to hide my sordid past.''

She left the window and walked back to the sofa. Once there she plopped down next to Anna Jane and sighed dramatically. "My sisters and I were on television when we were kids."

Anna Jane's eyes widened. "Really?"

She nodded. "There used to be a program called 'The Sally McGuire Show.' The three of us played Sally, who was an orphan."

"You all played one person?"

"Yes. There are laws preventing children from working very long hours on a set, so having identical triplets helped with the filming of the show."

The girl clapped her hands together. "I want to see one."

Elissa glanced at Fallon. "Tell me they don't have cable on the island."

"They do, but only a few channels. I think we're safe."

Anna Jane leaned toward her. "Ariel—I mean, Fallon. It would be fun."

"I have to agree," Jarrett said, looking intrigued. "The shows sound like fun."

Kayla squeezed her eyes shut. "They're not. Trust me. We weren't very good actors and some of the scenes are really frightening."

"You were always terrific," her husband, Patrick, told her as he put his arm around her. "I enjoy watching those old shows."

"Me, too," Cole agreed, smiling at his wife. "Better than home movies."

"Fortunately we're on a very small island," Elissa remarked. "There isn't a single video store for miles."

Fallon could see Jarrett's mind already at work. "Don't be so sure," she said. "My host has the ability to make things happen. Don't challenge him on this or we'll be buried in videos.''

"Too late," he told her.

"Great."

Jarrett pushed to his feet. "I'm sure you want a chance to catch up with each other, so I'll leave you alone for a little while. But I hope you'll do me the honor of joining my niece and me for dinner."

Her sisters looked at her and Fallon nodded. Elissa spoke for them. "We'd be delighted. Thank you for inviting us and for taking care of our sister."

"It was my pleasure. Now, if you'll excuse me, I'll go tell Leona that you'll be joining us."

He was dressed casually in jeans and a polo shirt, yet he had a presence. Fallon found herself proud of him and wanting to show him off. As if he was somehow connected to her.

"I want to tell Jarrett something," Fallon said, standing and going after him. "I'll be right back."

She hurried from the room and caught him in the foyer. "Jarrett?"

He turned. "Did they change their minds?"

She came to a stop in front of him. His dark hair was brushed back, although a few strands had fallen forward across his forehead. She wished she could push them into place.

"No," she told him. "I just wanted to thank you for inviting them. It's great to have them back in my life and I would have hated to not eat dinner with them when they went back to the—"

She stopped in midsentence as she realized what she was saying. "Oh, my. I guess I wasn't thinking." Now that her sisters were here, there was no reason to stay with Jarrett. When her sisters went back to the hotel, she would be going back with them.

The thought caused a sharp pain in her midsection. In all the excitement, she'd forgotten what finding her family meant—leaving Jarrett and Anna Jane. She would miss them so much.

Her mind continued to race, but she realized he was waiting for her to continue her train of thought. "Anyway, it was nice of you to have them stay."

"No problem," he told her. "Are you doing all right? This is a lot to take in."

"I know. I still can't believe it."

"Anything different?"

"Yeah, my clothes." She tugged on the hem of the cropped T-shirt. "I'm not usually such a casual dresser."

"It looks good on you."

His compliment made her flush. "Thank you."

"You seem to have kept your 'Ariel' memories."

"I have. I can recall everything about waking up here. It's strange to remember not remembering. I'm a little out of sorts, as if I haven't quite come back into focus, but I think that will just take time."

"You want me to call the doctor?"

"It's not that serious."

"If it changes, let me know."

"Promise."

She was barefoot, so he towered over her by several inches. She had to look up to meet his gaze. She studied his handsome features, wondering how long it would take to forget him. What would her ordinary world be like without Jarrett to brighten it?

"You must be happy to find out you have family," he said. "You were worried about being alone."

"I am pleased."

"Is there a husband or a couple dozen kids waiting for you somewhere?"

He asked the question lightly, yet she sensed the answer was important to him. Or maybe that was just wishful thinking on her part.

"I'm not married," she told him. "There isn't anyone in my life right now." The truth was, there had been boyfriends in the past, but no one important.

"Then I'll tell Leona we're going to be seven for dinner."

As he walked to the kitchen, Fallon stared after him. She'd found her family, but not someone special to care about her. Funny that it had never bothered her before, but now she knew being self-sufficient wasn't going to be as wonderful or fulfilling as it had been in the past.

After dinner, conversation continued to flow around the table. Jarrett listened more than he talked as the sisters caught each other up on everything that had happened while they'd been apart.

He was amazed at how easily they communicated, barely having to finish sentences before another of the women picked up the train of thought. He and Tracy had gotten along while they were growing up, but they'd never been close. Perhaps it was the difference in their ages, or the fact that their house had been large enough for them to go their separate ways. For the first time ever, he felt a sense of loss about that. It would have been nice for him and his sister to have been friends as well as family.

His gaze drifted from Fallon to Kayla and finally to Elissa. Odd that three women who looked so much alike could be so different. Even if he closed his eyes, he would be able to tell them apart. It wasn't just the words that they used, but also the cadence of their voices and the patterns of their speech.

He returned his attention to Fallon. She listened intently to her sisters, smiling at the appropriate time. He knew she was pleased to have her memory restored, and she claimed to feel all right, yet occasionally confusion crossed her face. He wondered if she was having trouble adjusting.

"They're like this all the time," Cole said, leaning toward his host. "Put the three of them together and you can't get a word in edgewise."

Patrick grinned. "It's true. I've given up trying to participate in conversations."

"So what do you think of our ladies?" Cole asked.

"They're very special," Jarrett told him. "Fallon was concerned that she was going to spend the rest of her life alone. I'm glad she has people who obviously care about her."

Patrick shook his head. He was a tall man, with blond hair and blue eyes. Fallon had told Jarrett that Patrick was a vet in San Diego. "I'm glad you were here to take care of her. None of us want anything to happen to any of them." He grimaced. "You're not going to let us pay you for your trouble, are you?"

"It wasn't any trouble," Jarrett said. "We've enjoyed having her around."

Cole raised his eyebrows but didn't say anything. No doubt the other man was wondering about the nature of his relationship with his sister-in-law. Jarrett would have told him—had he been able to figure it out himself.

Fallon wasn't the only one wrestling with confusion. He didn't know what to make of this turn of events. A few hours ago Fallon had been Ariel—a woman with no past and an unknown future. Who was she now? While he knew Ariel, he didn't know Fallon Bedford. Were they the same woman?

Ironically, he'd decided to trust Ariel and to graciously continue to share his life with her. He'd had grand plans to show her a good time for the holidays by giving her a place to belong. But she already had a place, and people who cared about her. She didn't need him.

Until the opportunity was gone, he hadn't realized how much he'd enjoyed being needed or how he'd wanted to make this time special for her.

Anna Jane got up from her seat and came around to his chair. "I'm going up to bed," she said.

He touched her cheek. She'd been quiet all during dinner.

"Do you want me to come with you and tuck you in?" he asked.

She nodded.

He rose to his feet and held out his hand. "I'm going to put Anna Jane to bed," he informed everyone at the table. "Why don't you move to the living room? It's more comfortable."

"Night, Anna Jane," Fallon said.

The child tightened her grip on Jarrett but didn't respond. She kept walking toward the door.

Jarrett glanced back and caught Fallon's surprised look. He shrugged, telling her he didn't know what was wrong, either.

Should he ask her, he wondered as they silently climbed the stairs. Should he scold her for being rude?

"Anna Jane, I know you're upset about Fallon's family returning," he started. "It's been a big shock. But you shouldn't ignore her like that. It's not nice."

They'd nearly reached the top of the stairs. Anna Jane

was one step ahead of him. She paused. "I—I know," she said, her voice cracking.

He bent close to her and saw tears streaming down her face. It was as if someone had sliced him open. He nearly groaned at the pain of seeing her hurt. Not knowing what else to do, he pulled her hard against his chest and hugged her.

"Hush, sweetie. It's all right."

"No, it's n-not," she sobbed, burying her face in his shoulder. "She's going away. She has her sisters and she doesn't need us anymore. I thought she'd be here for Christmas, but now she won't and I'll m-miss her."

She cried as if her heart were broken. Jarrett swore silently. It probably was. This was one more loss in the young girl's life. Considering all she'd been through in such a short period of time, she was amazingly normal.

He carried her into her room and sat on her bed. She clung to him. He held her tightly, rocking back and forth. "Anna Jane, I'm right here. We're going to be fine. I promise."

His gut continued to twist with pain—both for her and himself. He, too, would miss Fallon when she left them.

"I want her to stay for Christmas," Anna Jane cried.

"Me, too."

He wanted that more than he was willing to admit. But even if she left, she would leave behind a precious gift. She had shown him how to care about his niece. For the first time since her arrival, he was fiercely glad he was Anna Jane's guardian.

Chapter Ten

Fallon tried to concentrate on the conversation in the living room, but again and again her thoughts drifted upstairs to Anna Jane. Jarrett had been gone nearly an hour. The little girl had obviously been upset when she'd left the table. She hadn't even said good-night. Fallon tried not to take it personally, but that was hard. Finally she gave up trying to pretend and excused herself.

"Is everything all right?" Elissa asked.

"I hope so," Fallon answered. "Anna Jane wasn't herself at dinner. She's not usually that quiet."

"You and she were friends," Cole said. "Now she's afraid that's changed."

"Plus you're a real person, not someone she created from her imagination," Kayla added. "She's probably wondering if you're going to act differently."

"I'm sure you're right. I'll be back, guys."

Kayla took a sip of her water and sighed. "Take your

time. I'm not really the live-in-luxury type, but this house is fabulous. I can't believe you've been staying here."

Fallon glanced around at the expensively furnished room.

"Me, either." She smiled and left the room.

Once in the foyer, she paused at the bottom of the stairs and thought about the child who put notes in bottles and worried about creatures waiting to nip at her heels. While she'd still been Ariel, and desperate to get her memory back, she hadn't thought through what that would mean. That she would then be forced to leave. Having someone to care about her was wonderful, but she wished there was a way to have that and a place here, too. At least for a little while.

Her desire to stay wasn't just about herself. She also worried about Anna Jane and what their parting would mean to her. She'd already lost so many people in her life.

"You're looking serious about something."

She jumped at the sound of Jarrett's voice and glanced up as he started down the stairs.

"I was thinking about Anna Jane. Is she all right?"

"She's asleep."

"That doesn't answer my question." She folded her arms across her chest. "She's upset because I have a family and a life, isn't she?"

He reached the bottom of the stairs and touched her chin. "She's upset because you're leaving."

Fallon swallowed hard. "I was just thinking about that myself. When I lost my memory, all I wanted was to get it back. I wanted to know who I was and that there were people who cared about me."

"Now you know."

"I thought I would be happier," she admitted, trying

to ignore the sensual stroking of his fingers on her cheek. She was sure he didn't mean the contact to be erotic, but already her body warmed as a tingling swept through her.

"I'm not saying I'm not grateful that my family is here," she added quickly. "I love my sisters and I've missed them. I just wish..." She shrugged. "I don't know."

He sat on the bottom step and patted the space next to him. She sank down and drew her legs close to her chest.

"Why did you three pick St. Alicia?" he asked. "It's not a typical resort."

Fallon smiled at the memory. "It was my decision. My fifth graders were studying Caribbean history, so I had collected a lot of information, including travel brochures so they could have an idea of what the islands look like. The travel agent included a brochure for your resort, and I was hooked the first time I saw it."

She wrapped her arms around her knees. "My sisters had told me to pick the place I wanted to go. You see, the three of us have always traveled together. We used to take camping trips in college, long weekends. Always on a budget, of course. This was going to be our first five-star vacation."

His expression was unreadable. "You saved your pennies?"

"Not exactly. We, um, sort of got an inheritance."

"Really?"

She nodded. "Money from 'The Sally McGuire Show' was put into a trust fund until we turned twenty-five. That happened this past summer. Compared to your fortune, it's spare change, but it's enough for us. I planned to give some of mine to charity, to use some for travel and to invest the rest for my future."

He tucked her hair behind her ear. "So you weren't after my money at all."

"Nope. Sorry."

"I'm not."

The air around them crackled with an electrical charge. The tingling in her body intensified. Fallon wondered what would happen if she swayed toward him. Would he kiss her? Would she be able to keep from throwing herself at him?

"I have something to ask you," he said. His dark eyes pulled her in. She could no more look away than she could survive without breath.

"Uh-huh."

"Would you and your family consider spending your holidays here instead of at the hotel? There's plenty of room, and both Anna Jane and I would be pleased to have the company."

The invitation both shocked and thrilled her. "I don't know what to say."

"There's the pool and the beach. Leona is a great cook, as you know. If it will help, I'm not above using my niece to get what I want," he warned. "This would mean a lot to her."

"I know. I was thinking about her, too." She considered the possibility. Staying here for Christmas would be terrific. She could be with her sisters and still spend time with Jarrett and Anna Jane. "I love the idea, but I have to ask everyone else."

"No problem. I'll be in my office," he said. "You can let me know the decision. Please don't worry if you would rather return to the hotel. We'll both understand."

He might, but Anna Jane wouldn't, and neither would she. She *wanted* her time with them to continue. This wasn't real life, and eventually she was going to have to give up the fantasy and go home, but she wasn't ready to do that yet.

They both stood. "I'll be there in a few minutes," she promised, and crossed to the living room. As she entered, she took in the scene. The beautiful room, her sisters and their husbands talking together.

"There we were," Kayla said. "Ready to leave for the airport and I was running for the bushes."

"Thanks for that visual," Cole said dryly.

Kayla wrinkled her nose at her brother-in-law. "I warn you, Cole. Elissa and I are identical in many ways. That means if I have morning sickness, she's probably going to have it, too."

Cole paled at the thought. Elissa chuckled. "Don't worry, honey, I'll survive."

"I won't," he told her.

"I can handle Kayla's morning sickness," Patrick said, taking his wife's hand in his and kissing her palm. "What I can't understand is how she can be so cheerful afterward."

Fallon touched a hand to her flat belly and wondered what it would be like to carry a life inside her body. It must be a magical and humbling experience.

Elissa glanced up and saw her. "Is everything better?" she asked.

"She's sleeping, so I didn't get to talk with her," Fallon said. "I'll try tomorrow." She shoved her hands into her shorts pockets. "Speaking of which, I want to talk to you guys about something."

Kayla and Elissa shared a look. Fallon wondered what they'd been talking about.

"Jarrett has invited us to spend the holidays with him, here at the house." She held up her hand. "Before you say anything, I want to let you know that there's plenty of room and there's a pool and a private beach outside."

She paused, not sure how to phrase the rest of it. "Anna Jane and I have become friends. She's a sweet child, and in the past few months she's lost both her mother and her nanny who was her companion for most of her life. She's been here on the island less than a month and she's feeling a little lost. I know it would mean a lot to her to have company for the holidays. Not that I'm trying to make you feel guilty or anything."

"Right," Cole said dryly. "A lonely child *and* the great beachfront mansion. Tough decision."

"Ah, the rough life," Kayla said lightly.

"Be serious, you two," Elissa ordered, and turned to Fallon. "Wouldn't we be a bother? The size of the house party is going to more than double. I'm concerned about cooking for that many, not to mention providing food. We would have to offer Jarrett something in return."

"Don't try money," Patrick said. "He won't take it."

Kayla grinned. "I suspect our host is already getting everything he wants."

Fallon felt herself flush. "You couldn't be more wrong."

"Oh, I doubt it. The unflappable Fallon is starting to show a little wear around the edges. Is that your control I see unraveling?"

"If it is, it's because I've had amnesia for the past several days."

"Oh, I think it's more than that."

Fallon ignored her and looked at Elissa. "There's a full-time housekeeper here," she said. "But I agree with you on the cooking. Maybe we could pitch in. Or would that make it less like a vacation?"

Elissa glanced at her husband and brother-in-law, then

at Kayla. "We're not going to turn our back on Anna Jane," she declared. "Not after she and Jarrett have taken care of you. Besides, the little girl seems very sweet and we would love to make her holiday special. We know what it's like to lose a parent."

Fallon winced as she remembered that first Christmas after their father had died. Their mother had seemed very comfortable with her new husband, but the triplets had suffered through missing him.

"We don't need convincing," Patrick said. "We'd love to stay, and we'll help where we can. Frankly, I prefer the idea of Christmas in someone's home rather than in the resort. It's more personal."

Her sisters nodded. "Then it's settled," Cole stated. "Tell our host we'd be delighted to accept his invitation."

"Thanks," Fallon murmured, and left the room. She should have known. Once she explained the situation, there wouldn't ever have been a question of them not staying. They were wonderful people and she was lucky to be a part of this family.

Anna Jane would have her happy Christmas, the triplets and their spouses would be together, and Fallon got to spend more time with Jarrett. All in all, it was what the business world referred to as a win-win situation.

But the pleasure at staying didn't explain the rapid patter of her heart, nor the fluttering in the pit of her stomach. Somehow she knew she was getting the best part of the deal. Even better, she wasn't even going to complain.

She stopped in the doorway to Jarrett's office. He was working at his computer. The sun had already set and the bare windows reflected the scene, the mirror image capturing his intensity as well as his good looks. What odd quirk of fate had brought her into this man's world? Under ordinary circumstances, they would never have crossed paths. She knew that after the holidays she would leave this place and never return. Would he think of her? Would he remember these weeks, when a letter in a bottle had invited a strange woman to share his life? Would he remember her? She had a feeling that she would never forget him, no matter who else might enter her life.

"Jarrett?"

He glanced up. She felt the impact of his gaze all the way to her toes. It was as if she'd suddenly stepped very close to a fire. Heat flared across her body, making her breasts swell and her thighs tremble.

"What's the verdict?"

"We would love to stay. Thank you for having us."

"The pleasure is all mine."

She knew for a fact that wasn't true, but it was nice of him to say. "When you tell Leona, don't let her panic. We'll all be happy to pitch in. My sisters and I are pretty decent in the kitchen. Nothing fancy, but we can do the basic stuff."

He shook his head and rose to his feet. "That isn't necessary. Leona has easily handled house parties four times this size. That's one of her major complaints about working with me. She doesn't have enough to do. She'll be thrilled with the opportunity to show off her skills."

"We're the ones who are thrilled," she said, trying not to sound breathless as he made his way toward her. His lean body moved with perfect grace. "The house is so beautiful, as are the beach and pool. Everyone will have a great time. Anna Jane gets company. It's perfect." She licked her lips nervously as he drew closer. "I'll remind everyone to keep the noise down so you can work."

"Don't worry about that."

He stopped in front of her and braced one hand on the door frame by her head. She was closed in on three sides. It would have been easy to slide away, but she didn't want to. She liked Jarrett being close to her. She could inhale the scent of him. Two parts tantalizing masculine fragrance, one part something mysterious and uniquely him.

His gaze flickered over her face. She felt it as tangibly as a touch. "Thank you," she said.

"You just did."

The handsome planes of his face, the dark eyes and firm mouth all made it impossible to concentrate. "Not just for the invitation," she explained, "but for the way you asked. You questioned me to find out about my plans. Obviously you didn't want to interfere if we had something we already wanted to do."

He shrugged. "I was afraid you would feel obligated because of your relationship with Anna Jane."

"She's not an obligation."

"Now it's my turn to thank you. For caring about her."

"I'm a teacher," Fallon said. "That's my job."

"You did it before you knew you were a teacher. I don't think it's your job as much as who you are."

Fallon had the oddest feeling they were, in fact, having a conversation about something else entirely. But she didn't know what, or if she was just reacting to his nearness. He was close enough that if she wanted to, she could have slid her arms around his waist and leaned against him.

Lord, how she wanted to. She wanted him to hold her, too, to kiss her and—

"I'll notify the hotel and tell them to collect your things and send all of the luggage over."

She blinked, trying to figure out what he was talking about. Oh, the luggage. Obviously he wasn't fighting the same desire she was.

"Um, sure. Wait. I'd better go over so I can make sure everything of mine gets packed. Elissa and Kayla will want to come with me to make sure they collect all of their luggage, too. Is there a car?"

He nodded. "A van. Frank will drive you."

But he made no move to call Frank. Instead he moved a half step closer. They were nearly touching.

"Fallon, I..."

Instead of finishing his sentence, he lowered his head and brushed her mouth with his. The kiss was soft and sweet. Passion flared, but it was the quiet kind, as if her body knew that family was in the other room and nothing could happen between them right now. But there was always later.

The thought made her surge up against him, returning his pressure and increasing it. She rested her fingertips on his shoulders. A groan caught in his throat and the sound thrilled her to her bones.

He pulled away slowly and stared at her. She basked in the fire reflected in his gaze, drawing strength from the heat. He touched her cheek. "I'll go call Frank," he said, and turned away.

Her eyes burned. She couldn't figure out what was wrong, then she realized she was very close to tears. Which was strange. She never cried.

Jarrett waited patiently on hold while the woman on the other end of the phone looked up the information. The music was silenced as a voice said, "Yes, sir, we have those videos in stock. Where did you need them shipped?''

He gave her an address in St. Thomas, knowing it would be quicker to have them delivered there and then brought to the island. After giving his credit card number, he hung up and crossed off the item on his list.

When packages had to be air-expressed to St. Thomas, shopping this late was expensive, but he didn't have much choice. He hadn't known about his houseful of company in time to plan a trip to the stores. Besides, he had made millions of dollars in the past few years. This house had been his only extravagance. He rarely spent money otherwise. If not for Anna Jane, Fallon and her family, then for whom?

The front door opened and he heard the sound of voices, laughter and footsteps. Everyone had decided to accompany Frank back to the hotel. He'd heard a spirited argument about whether or not all the people plus the luggage would fit in the van. A friendly debate had broken out between the men and women about how much luggage was actually required for a vacation of this kind.

"I can carry my own bags," Fallon protested from the foyer.

"No problem," Frank told her. "Mr. Jarrett told me to take care of you. That's what I'm doing."

"Dammit, Kayla, you're pregnant. Don't pick up a suitcase," her husband demanded.

"It's just a little one."

"Put it down now."

"Don't have a cow, Patrick. I'm pregnant, not incapacitated."

"I'm not going to think of touching luggage," Elissa said, and laughed. "So don't look at me like that."

There was no response from Cole, but Jarrett could picture his stern expression.

These sounds showed him that over the years his beautiful tropical prison had become a silent place. In the past few weeks he'd had only the sounds of Anna Jane's footsteps to liven his world. Listening to the banter of the triplets and their husbands, he realized his niece had been far too quiet. No wonder she felt isolated. He should have noticed sooner. He didn't want his home to be a prison for her, too.

He would have to do something. After the first of the year, he would think about making some changes. But what? He still couldn't forget the past. He still couldn't bring himself to trust. Were trusting and possibly caring even wise?

He remembered Tracy's pain when her husband had been killed. She'd broken down at the funeral, begging God to take her, too. When Donald died, Tracy's life had ended. He, Jarrett, didn't ever want to be in that position.

More laughter filtered through his half-open door. He easily picked out Fallon's and smiled. He was glad she was staying. Had she guessed the truth? Did she know that he'd shamelessly used Anna Jane as the excuse for asking her stay, when he'd really wanted her to stay for himself? He could *think* that he wanted her here, but he could never risk telling her.

How would she feel if she knew he'd asked her stay for himself and not for the child?

He closed his eyes and recalled the sweetness of her lips touching his. He shouldn't have kissed her. Yet, short of dying, nothing could have stopped him. He needed her.

Jarrett opened his eyes and straightened. No. Not *needed*. Never needed. Wanted. There was a difference.

He wanted her and he liked her. That's as much as he was willing to admit. He'd grown fond of his mystery woman. Only she wasn't a mystery anymore. She had an identity and a past. How was that going to change her?

Chapter Eleven

Fallon stuck out her tongue at her reflection. "You're not helping," she told the mirror.

A soft giggle came from behind her. She shifted and saw Anna Jane standing in the doorway to her bedroom. "You're talking to yourself," the girl said.

"I know. The worst part is I keep waiting for an answer, but there isn't one."

Anna Jane's face was bright and smiling this morning. She skipped into the room and wrapped her arms around Fallon's waist. "I'm glad you're staying," she said.

Fallon set her brush on the dresser and touched the child's head. "Me, too. It's going to be a great Christmas."

Anna Jane looked up at her. "Why were you talking to yourself?"

"I can't decide how to wear my hair." Fallon turned

back to her reflection. "There's the Ariel way and the Fallon way."

"How are they different?"

"Fallon is a lot more boring," she said truthfully. "Neat, tidy and sensible. Ariel wore her hair up on her head or loose or—" She shrugged. "I can't decide what to do."

"But you're Ariel, too. She's not a different person, she's just you with no memory."

Fallon figured Ariel had a lot more excitement in her life than Fallon ever had. "You're right," she agreed, and started pinning her hair up on top of her head. So what if it wasn't her usual style? It was still flattering. She was on vacation—why not have a little fun?

"What are you up to this morning?" she asked Anna Jane.

"I'm going to show Elissa and Kayla the beach where I found you."

"That should be interesting."

The girl nodded. "It's nice that they look like you. Even though I don't know them, I like them. Because of you."

Her words touched Fallon. She dropped to a crouch. "I like you, too," she said, tugging on a strand of dark hair. "A lot. You have fun with them."

"You could come with us."

"I have to unpack." She pointed to the large suitcase and garment bag by the closet.

"What about the clothes Uncle Jarrett gave you?"

"I still have them." In fact, she was wearing a pair of shorts and a T-shirt from his boutique right now. "I need to go through my things to reconnect with who I am," Fallon said. "I've remembered everything, but I haven't been myself for a long time."

"I understand." Anna Jane nodded solemnly.

"I'll see you at lunch," she told the girl. "Have a good time this morning."

"We will." The nine-year-old gave her a quick wave and dashed out of the room.

Fallon rose to her feet and approached her luggage. She probably should have unpacked last night, but she'd put off the task. Mostly because going through her things at the hotel had given her an odd feeling. While her clothes and belongings had been familiar as she'd packed them for the move, they had also been faintly strange. It was almost as if she'd found an old box full of high school mementos. While the individual items brought back memories, they belonged to a different time and place.

"It's just clothes," she told herself as she hung her garment bag on the back of the door.

She unzipped the top flap and began removing her things. She'd brought a couple of summer dresses. The neutral colors—beige and gray blue—surprised her. While she remembered buying the dresses and even wearing them last summer, they didn't feel as if they belonged to her. When she hung them in the closet, they didn't fit in with the brightly colored garments already there.

She fingered the skirt she'd chosen from the clothes Jarrett had sent over. The dark green silk was the same color as her eyes. The matching blouse was sleeveless and sexy. Together the outfit created a casual elegance combining soft, flowing fabric and hints at the feminine shape beneath. The two dresses she'd brought with her were...sensible. The tailored style was classic. With a light jacket she could easily wear either to school or a lunch. Yet when placed next to the green outfit, the dresses nearly blended with the wall paint.

She walked to her suitcase and picked it up. After placing it on the bed, she unfastened the catches and flipped it open. More sensible clothing lay there. Tailored shirts and shorts. White cotton underwear. She thought about the lacy bra she currently wore and the high-cut legs on her panties, then fingered the plain straps of her white bra. She picked up a cream short-sleeved shirt and held it in front of her. Then she turned to the mirror. Today she wore a red T-shirt and white shorts. The shorts were casual with an elastic waist and tiny slits on the thighs. The button-front camp shirt she held didn't belong to this new person, yet it was in her luggage.

Fallon dropped it back on the bed and stared at her belongings. How could she remember owning them, recover her memory and have them not feel right? Could being Ariel have changed her that much?

Or had the memory loss simply allowed another side of her personality to come out? Maybe because she hadn't had to be so busy running around taking care of everyone, she'd finally been free to be herself.

She bent over and began pulling things out of her suitcase. Books, a bag of cosmetics, her blow dryer. There was the beautiful bottle Anna Jane had used to send the note. Then her fingers touched something hard. She pulled out a slim leather-bound book. Her journal.

Fallon sank onto the bed. Inside these pages were her hopes and dreams. She'd never kept long entries, but she'd made it a habit to jot down odd notes about her life or what she wanted from the future. She flipped through a few pages, stopping to read an account of picking out St. Alicia as the family's holiday destination. What a happy quirk of fate. No matter what happened when she left, she promised herself she would never regret being here.

Another entry caught her eye. It was dated at the end of summer, just after she and her sisters had come into their trust fund.

August 25th: I must come to some decision about my future. I want to travel, but I'll need a plan for when I return. What is it to be? Grad school for an advanced degree? Do I want to return to teaching at the elementary school? I've thought about opening my own business. By the time I return from my sabbatical, I'll have made up my mind which it's to be. The world is filled with possibilities and I don't want to miss any of them.

Fallon read the entry a second time. Hopes and plans for the future. But instead of feeling excited, she was startled by a whisper of sadness. Maybe because reading it these months later she saw something she hadn't seen when she'd first made the entry. All her plans had one basic assumption—that she would be alone. There was no mention of a man in her journal, no thought of falling in love and how that would affect her future. When she returned from her sabbatical, no one would be waiting. No one, except her sisters, would miss her, or even think about her.

Fallon remembered that she'd always valued being independent and self-sufficient. With her two sisters to worry about, she'd respected those qualities in herself. Now, with her whole life stretching out in front of her, she wondered about being alone...and lonely.

"You're looking serious about something."

She glanced up and saw Jarrett standing in the open

doorway. She smiled. "I found my journal and am rediscovering myself."

"Any surprises?"

"A couple."

"Pleasant ones, I hope."

She shrugged, but didn't answer.

He stepped inside. While he usually wore jeans around the house, today he was dressed in shorts and a T-shirt. His legs were long, muscular and tanned. She found herself in danger of being mesmerized by his powerful thighs.

He pulled out the stool in front of the dresser and sat down. "So who is Fallon Bedford?"

"Someone very different from the mysterious Ariel."

"I don't think I believe that."

"It's true." She pointed to the open closet. "See those two dresses hanging there? Compare them to the skirt. They have nothing in common. Everything I chose from what the boutique sent over is different from what I owned before." She dropped her journal onto the bed, then touched her head. "I wasn't sure how to fix my hair this morning. When I was first here I was frustrated because I couldn't remember how I used to wear it. Now I can't decide if I still want to wear it that way."

He nodded. "You're having trouble fitting back into your own skin."

"Exactly."

"It'll take a few days to adjust, but you'll do it. Do you want me to have the doctor stop by?"

"Physically, I'm fine."

His gaze lightly touched on her body. Instantly the heat in the room went up several degrees. "If I agree with that last statement, will you slap me?" he asked teasingly.

She felt a blush on her cheeks. "No."

"Good." He grinned. "I'm just trying to be agreeable." He pointed to her suitcase. "Maybe losing your memory just brought out another side of your personality."

"I'm sure that's it, but it's still weird to think there are parts of me I didn't know existed."

"We all have pieces locked away."

"How do I put them back?"

"Do you want to?" he asked.

She thought about the question. "Actually, I don't. I think I liked Ariel quite a bit. The trick is going to be making her fit in with the old Fallon."

"Will the new Fallon be a compromise between the two?"

"I hope so." She grabbed a plain beige T-shirt and wrinkled her nose. "Although I might have to get rid of some of the old Fallon's sensible clothes. Oh!" She looked at him. "I nearly forgot. Who do I talk to about paying for my new clothes? I have credit cards and money now."

He shook his head. "No charge."

"Jarrett, you have to let me pay. Something tells me you won't let us reimburse you for staying here over the holidays—although we're really going to try. You have to let me give you something."

Instead of answering, he rose to his feet and held out his hand. Fallon let the T-shirt fall, offered him her fingers and let him pull her to her feet. Together they crossed to the window.

From her bedroom they could see a bit of the pool and all of the beach beyond. He opened the window. Over the sound of waves came a high-pitched squeal of laughter. Seconds later Anna Jane bounded into view. Elissa and Kayla were with her. Each of the women had hold of one of her hands. While Fallon couldn't hear their conversation, she knew the trio was having fun.

"I couldn't have given her that," Jarrett said. "You taught me what she needed, and I think the two of us are going to be okay now. I owe you, Fallon. So, no, you can't pay for your clothes or for staying here. You've given me more than I can ever repay."

"I'm happy I could help, but you're making it more than it was."

His dark eyes flared bright. "No. I'm not."

He hadn't released her fingers. She told herself it was because he'd forgotten he was holding them, but *she* hadn't forgotten. Not for a second. Even now she could feel the broadness of his palm and the strength of him. Jarrett Wilkenson was going to be a tough act for any man to follow.

"Anna Jane is very glad you're staying," he said.

"I know. I'm glad, too." Was he? He didn't say and she didn't ask. Fear held her back. Would Ariel have asked? Probably not, Fallon decided, but she might have hinted. Ariel had definitely been the more courageous of the two. She frowned. She'd better stop thinking of herself as two people or she would end up locked away in some institution after having been diagnosed with multiple personality disorder. The thought made her smile.

She glanced at Jarrett to see if he'd noticed her humor, but his attention was focused on the beach. She followed his gaze and saw that he was staring at her sisters. They'd linked arms and were walking together as Anna Jane chased the tide.

"The three of you are very close," he said.

"We always have been. It's a triplet thing. We often know what the others are thinking. In some ways our personalities are very different, but in others, they're exactly the same.''

"I envy you that."

"Weren't you close with your sister?"

He shrugged. "Not really. Tracy was older. We grew up in a big house. It was too big. We were in separate wings and didn't spend much time together. Looking back, I wish it had been different. We didn't have much in common. Maybe if we'd tried we might have been more a part of each other's lives.''

"Would you have liked that?"

His gaze never left her sisters. "A month ago I would have said no. Now I'm not so sure. I'm beginning to see what I missed."

Without thinking, she squeezed his fingers. The action was fraught with peril. After all, she'd just reminded him they were still holding hands. But instead of pulling back, he returned the pressure of her touch and drew her a little closer.

Their shoulders brushed. She felt his heat and wanted to be closer still. But this time it wasn't about sex. Although she wanted him, her desire for nearness was more about caring and comfort than passion.

"She must have been great," Fallon said softly. "Look at Anna Jane. She's a terrific kid."

"How much of that was Tracy and how much Nana B.?" he asked. "My sister had many good qualities, but she wasn't much of a hands-on mother. Her relationship with her husband consumed her. It was as if they were the only two people in the world."

"Is that bad?" she asked, wondering what it must be like to be loved that much. She'd had a few boyfriends, but never true love.

"I think so," he said. "They loved each other to the

exclusion of their child. I would think the best kind of love would make room for other people." He grimaced. "But then, I'm not an expert."

She thought about what he'd said. "You're right," she told him. "My sisters are like that. They adore their husbands, but there is room in each of their lives for other people. They'll both make great mothers."

Jarrett released her hand. Before she had a chance to protest or feel lonely, he touched her cheek. "You will, too. You already have all the best qualities. Affection, patience, a great sense of timing. You fell into my world right when I needed you most. I hate to think how Anna Jane would have spent this Christmas if you hadn't showed up."

His sweet touch made her ache. She *wanted* him to think she was special. "You two would have muddled through."

"She needs more than muddling right now." He lowered his hand to his side and glanced out the window. "Have you ever been in love?" he asked. "Not like my sister and her husband, but just in love?"

"No. You?"

An odd expression flickered across his face, then was gone. She remembered the hints about a mysterious romantic past from the magazine articles.

"You don't have to answer that," she told him. "I didn't mean to pry. It's not important."

"It's not that," he said. "I generally don't talk about the past with many people. But it might explain some things about me. Like why I acted the way I did when you were found on the beach. Did I ever apologize for that?"

She shook her head.

"I'm sorry, Fallon. I should have believed you."

"No, you shouldn't have. Because of who you are and what you've accomplished, there are a lot of people trying to get a piece of you. You had no way of knowing I was any different. I completely understand."

He leaned against the window frame and crossed his arms over his chest. "If I were in your position, I don't think I'd be anywhere near this forgiving."

She smiled. "Yes, you would be. I'm sure of it."

"Do you trust the entire world?"

"Pretty much. I try not to be stupid, but I don't assume everyone is lying or out to get me."

His amusement faded. "Must be nice." He motioned to the bed. "It's a long story. You might want to have a seat."

She did as he requested and perched on the edge of the bed. Instead of joining her, or sitting on the stool, he continued to lean against the window. His gaze seemed to focus on a past she couldn't see.

"I think I already mentioned that my parents were killed when I was eighteen."

She nodded.

"My sister wasn't interested in running the empire. By that time she'd already found Donald, and nothing else mattered. So it fell on my shoulders."

"That's a lot for a kid to handle," she said, wondering what it must have been like to have inherited so much responsibility.

"Tell me about it. I wanted to make the family business a success. I figured the best way to do that was to go to college and learn as much as I could. I worked hard and got through in three years. Then I took over the hotel chain." He seemed to lose himself in the memories.

"I worked eighteen-hour days, seven days a week," he said. "I was too young and inexperienced to be scared, so I just plunged in with both feet. Sometimes I made mistakes, and sometimes I scored big. At the end of a couple of years I'd done more right than wrong and we were in the black. Four years later I'd created an empire.''

"I'm trying to picture what it must have been like and I can't,'' she said. "While I admire what you accomplished, I wonder at the cost. Did you ever have any fun?''

One eyebrow rose slightly. "Are you talking about fun or women?''

She smiled. "Both.''

"I got away on occasion, and I found out I was considered an eligible bachelor. Women were easy to get but hard to get rid of. Because I didn't have time to socialize very much, I was pretty inept.''

"I can't believe that.''

He looked at her and gave her a slow, sexy grin that made her toes curl. "Trust me.''

"Did you get your heart broken?''

"A couple of times. I thought they cared, but they only wanted money. So I pulled back. That fanned the fire. Women were everywhere. I was all of twenty-six or twenty-seven. I didn't want to make another mistake, but I wanted a woman in my life. So I started an affair with Charlotte, my personal secretary.''

Fallon was surprised at the flash of fire she felt rip through her. It took her a second to realize the heat didn't come from passion but was instead about jealousy.

Jarrett shook his head. "I had it all planned. She was a few years older, divorced and seemed as uninterested in an emotional commitment as I was. She made it easy. I could show up at the functions I had to attend, be the center of attention and leave alone. The affair lasted nearly two years."

"Did she continue to work for you?"

He nodded. "Like I said, I was pretty inept. But she was too good at her job. I didn't want to think about replacing her. Then one day I decided I wanted a real relationship. I wanted to date someone I could have a future with."

He paused. "I cared about Charlotte, but I never loved her. Sometimes having rules isn't enough."

"She'd fallen in love with you?" Fallon guessed.

"I don't know *what* it was. If that was love, I don't want any part of it. When I tried to break it off, she made things impossible around the office. I was forced to fire her. I tried to give her money, but she only wanted to be with me. She began stalking me." He shifted and shoved his hands into his shorts pockets. "I had to get a restraining order, but that wasn't enough. I moved twice, and each time she found me. She tried to destroy a couple of hotel deals. When she finally realized I wasn't going to take her back, she broke in to my house and set it on fire. She was caught in the blaze and died."

Fallon stared at him, not sure what to think. She'd expected some kind of tragedy in his past. A love affair gone wrong. But never this.

"How horrible," she said slowly.

"It was. I blamed myself for a long time, although except for not starting the affair, I'm not sure what I could have done differently. I lost lots of personal things in that fire. Pictures of my parents, a couple of collections that had meant a lot to me. Yet none of that mattered. In the end, I'd grown to hate Charlotte, yet I never wished her ill. I would have done anything to bring her back."

"That's when you moved here, isn't it?" she asked. "This is your refuge. They can't get to you here."

"Exactly. We'd just finished construction on the resort. It wasn't difficult to keep the workers around and build this house. They had it done in a couple of months. I've been here ever since."

"Do you ever go back to the States?"

"A few times a year. On business. I don't want to move back, though."

"I guess there are all those unhappy memories to deal with." She thought about what she'd heard. "There was very little in the articles. Did you deliberately keep the story from the press?"

"Yes. Charlotte had family. They'd tried to stop her, too. I didn't want to make it more difficult for them. My house was out in the country, so it's not as if she set Fifth Avenue on fire. I paid off a couple of reporters and that took care of it."

The woman had stalked Jarrett and made his life miserable, yet after her death he went out of his way to make sure her family wasn't haunted by the media. "No wonder she loved you," Fallon murmured.

"What?"

She shook her head. "Nothing. I was just thinking you were kind to her family."

"They hadn't done anything wrong. Why should they suffer, too?" He looked uncomfortable. "I didn't tell you this to get the sympathy vote, just to explain why I was a little paranoid when you first showed up."

She gazed at him, at the strength in his face, and the pain. For the first time since she'd met him, she could see the stark misery in his expression. It wasn't obvious, but its shadow lurked on the edges of his life.

"It does make sense, Jarrett. I appreciate you trusting

me with this information. You have my word I won't share it with anyone. Not even my sisters. I'm glad we cleared everything up and can be friends now.''

"Are we friends?"

The question surprised her. "I hope so."

"Me, too. Imagine my chagrin when you're not only *not* a gold digger, but you have an inheritance all your own.''

She smiled. "I think comparing my trust fund to your fortune is like comparing the acorn to the mighty oak, but it's enough for me.''

"What are you going to do when you leave here after Christmas?''

She hadn't thought that far ahead. Her first choice would be not to leave. Unfortunately, that wasn't one of the options. "I'd planned to travel. I'm on a year's sabbatical from teaching. When I finally go home I want to have made some plans for my future. Do I go back to teaching, do I get a higher degree, do I open my own business?''

"I know your sisters are heading back to the States on the thirtieth. Would you consider sticking around for another week or so? I'd like to pick your brain about Anna Jane, plus you're a fun houseguest.''

His casual invitation made her palms sweat. He actually wanted her to stay longer? She pressed her knees together to keep from jumping up and screaming "Yes!'' at the top of her lungs.

"I don't have to be anywhere specific,'' she said. "I would be happy to stay.'' Forever.

She pushed that last thought away. What did she know about forever? Jarrett was a relative stranger in her life. Just because he was charming, good-hearted, funny and handsome as sin didn't mean she could afford to lose her head. She needed to be rational about the whole thing. Which was hard to do when every cell in her body had broken into the "Hallelujah Chorus."

"Great," he responded simply.

Hoping her pleasure didn't show on her face, she said, "You'd better be careful, Jarrett. You continue to issue invitations, I might not want to leave."

"Would it be so bad if you got used to being around here?" he asked, then winked and walked out before she could catch her breath enough to answer.

Jarrett walked down the stairs toward his office. He half expected to be embarrassed by the fact that Fallon knew the worst about him, but instead he felt relieved. Oddly, he trusted her to understand. Maybe because she was basically a compassionate person. Look at how she acted with Anna Jane.

Is that why he'd asked her to stay after the holidays? The invitation had been impulsive, although he didn't regret it. If anything, he was pleased that she was going to be around. But shouldn't he *want* her gone? Shouldn't he be worried about her getting under his skin? After all, he knew better than most the price of getting involved.

He knew that love meant pain. Look at what had happened with Tracy when she'd lost Donald, and Anna Jane when she'd lost both her mother and her nanny. And what about Charlotte? Hadn't she paid the ultimate price for love?

He knew better than to risk caring and losing. Better to be alone. Better not to feel.

But not feeling had ceased to be an option in his life. While he had Fallon to blame for that, she wasn't the one he thought of. Instead, as he heard familiar footsteps in the foyer, he turned toward his niece and smiled.

She raced toward him. "Uncle Jarrett, I walked on the beach with Kayla and Elissa and we talked and I'm having the best time."

She launched herself at him. He caught her in midair and spun her around. "You're happy?"

She nodded and grinned. "Oh, yes. Very. This is going to be a wonderful Christmas." She leaned her head close to his ear. "You know, I was afraid you were gonna forget, but you didn't, did you?"

A sharp pain stabbed his heart. He very well might have forgotten, or at least not paid attention. If not for Fallon. Thank God she'd come into his life when she had.

He held Anna Jane next to him, feeling her small body. She would be a beautiful young woman in a few years, but for now she was still little enough to want hugs. He would make sure he gave her plenty.

She rested her head on his shoulder. "The nasty creatures are gone," she said as he sat on the bottom stair and settled her on his lap.

"What nasty creatures?"

"The ones that used to live down here. I could feel them watching me when I climbed the stairs alone. They scared me. I was afraid they were going to come after me, so I ran really fast to the top. Fallon said it was okay to have scary creatures, but to understand they couldn't really hurt me."

He looked down at her. "I wish you'd told me about them."

"I wanted to, but you were busy with your empire."

"Promise me the next time there's something scary, you come tell me no matter what. And the hell with my empire."

She looked up at him, her dark eyes wide and bright with humor. "Uncle Jarrett, that's a bad word."

"I know. Sorry. But do you promise?"

She nodded her head. "I'm glad they're gone, and I'm glad you're here." She squeezed him tight.

Sometime in the past few days he'd decided it was safe to love this child. She couldn't hurt him the way a woman could. She brought him love and laughter. But Fallon was the one who had brought color to his world. Before her, he'd lived in a drab place of grays. And he would return there when she left. Then he would be the one with creatures nipping at his heels. Better to be haunted by the vicious bites of imaginary creatures than risk the ultimate price of love.

Chapter Twelve

Fallon sat down on the lounge chair by the pool. Intellectually she knew that only a few hundred miles north, along the eastern seaboard, there were people shoveling snow. But here, in this tropical paradise, her heart found it hard to believe the entire world wasn't warm, sunny and tropical.

She adjusted the back of the chair so it lay more at an angle, then she stretched out her legs and closed her eyes. After a morning spent going through her luggage and trying to assimilate her brief time as the mysterious "Ariel" with her memories, she needed a break.

"Don't even think about going to sleep," a voice said.

Fallon opened her eyes and saw both her sisters looming over her. "Uh-oh. I recognize those looks," she said. "You guys are about to interrogate me. I should have guessed."

"Exactly," Kayla agreed, bending over and tugging

on Fallon's hand. "There's no point in resisting, so give in graciously when we tell you we're going for a walk on the beach."

Fallon rose to her feet and glanced around. "Where's Anna Jane?"

Elissa smiled. "Helping Leona with more baking. It was a tough decision for her, but Kayla and I convinced her we understood being torn between company and chocolate chip cookies. She could talk to us later in the day, so it was okay for the cookies to win."

They began walking in step, heading down to the beach. "She's wonderful," Kayla said. "She talked a little about missing her mother and her nanny. After all she's been through, it's amazing she's as well-adjusted as she is."

"Her uncle has something to do with that."

"And you." Kayla's gaze was knowing. "Every other sentence started with 'Fallon this' or 'Fallon always says.'"

Just thinking about Anna Jane made Fallon's heart tighten in her chest. "I really like her, too. Even when I couldn't remember who I was or if I had a family or children of my own, I felt drawn to her. She's a special child and I'm glad I've had a chance to get to know her."

They left the path and walked onto the sand. It was warm and smooth beneath her feet. To their left was the sea. A tropical breeze teased at them, bringing with it the scents of the island. She raised her face to the sun.

"Don't you love it here?" she asked. "I can't imagine wanting to spend Christmas anywhere else. It's not as traditional as a ski lodge, but it's still magic."

There was no reply. She glanced to her left, then to her right, suddenly realizing her sisters had neatly trapped her between them. Their expressions were identical—she had to cough up some information right now, or else.

She squared her shoulders. "What do you want to know?"

Kayla tossed her head. She wore her hair back in a ponytail, and the gold-blond strands danced with the movement. Her cutoff denim shorts exposed long, tanned legs. A loose white sleeveless blouse covered the bare hint of roundness in her belly.

"Start at the beginning," Kayla said. "You opened your eyes and saw this gorgeous guy staring down at you. There was instant attraction, and then?"

"Don't leave anything out," Elissa added. "We want details."

"There's nothing to tell," Fallon said.

Kayla chuckled. "We are more than your sisters, Fallon. We are your *identical* sisters. Don't try and pretend with us." Her voice dropped. "We have ways of making you talk," she intoned.

Fallon smiled. "I'm being serious. There isn't anything to tell. Jarrett is—" How did she describe him? What words could she use to define the complexity of their relationship?

"It's not what you think," she said at last. "He's been very kind."

"I've seen the way he looks at you," Elissa told her. "He's more than kind. He's interested. So, what's been happening?"

Stalling for time, Fallon paused and removed her sandals. Her sisters followed suit. Then they moved down to the water's edge. The sand was firm and damp, but still warm. As the gentle waves rushed over her feet, Fallon dug her toes in deep. Despite the fact that it was late December, the Caribbean Sea still felt like bathwater.

"I know you're hoping to hear some exciting, romantic story, but it isn't like that. When I was first found, Jarrett was a little concerned about me. He's very wealthy and very successful. Women have tried to get to him in very unethical ways."

Kayla's eyes widened. "He thought you were faking it?"

"It crossed his mind."

"But he quickly figured out the truth," Elissa added.

Fallon thought about those first few days. She wouldn't have used the word *quickly*, but she didn't really want to go into detail. "He made the decision to trust me," she said, because it was close to the truth. "We're friends. I like him. That's the end of it."

"Bummer," Kayla said. "I was hoping for a few details about hot kisses in the moonlight."

Fallon was careful to keep her expression neutral. "Sorry to disappoint you."

"Uh-huh."

She didn't dare look at either of them. They would know what she was thinking—worse, what she was trying to hide. While there hadn't been bunches of hot kisses, there had been that one evening. Just thinking about it made her start tingling. And the second she started to tingle, her sisters would know.

Elissa kicked at the water, then took a couple of steps back and sat on the sand. The skirt of her peach sundress billowed out around her. "You don't *just* like him, Fallon. I can see it, even if you can't."

Fallon plopped down next to her. "I'm not sure what I feel. These past twenty-four hours have been sort of strange. This time yesterday I didn't know who I was. Now my life is restored. I'm trying to make it all connect somehow."

Kayla waded out until the waves reached her knees. "What was losing your memory like?"

Fallon frowned. "Sort of like being in a mental tunnel. I knew what was going on around me, but I could only see directly in front. There were no sides, no points of reference. The worst part was wondering if I had any friends or family. There was no one looking for me at the resort. I spent a few nights thinking I didn't belong anywhere."

Elissa shuddered. "I don't ever want to know what that's like." She gave Fallon's arm a quick squeeze. "You have us, and you'll always have us."

"That's right," Kayla said. "You couldn't get rid of us even if you wanted to. You can run, but we'll track you down."

"You don't know how good that makes me feel."

Elissa studied her. "Do you feel any different because of your experience?"

"A little. When I didn't know who I was, I wasn't just Fallon with no memory. I changed."

Kayla looked at her. "How?"

"My clothes." Fallon pointed to her cropped red T-shirt and shorts. "Did you notice what I'm wearing? It's not conservative, it's not tailored. When I opened my suitcase, I was shocked by what I saw there. Everything is familiar, but it doesn't look right. Even though I can remember wearing those things, I don't want to put them on now. I'm wearing my hair loose, the makeup isn't the same. I feel slightly out of focus somehow."

"Maybe it's just a different side of your personality coming out," Elissa said. "You've always been the responsible one, Fallon. I assumed the reason you dressed so conservatively was because you were trying to look more in charge. I don't know if it's because you are the oldest, or it's just a quirk of your personality, but for some reason, you are the leader of the three of us. You've spent a lot of time worrying about us, which hasn't left all that much time for yourself."

"Someone had to take care of things," Fallon grumbled, reasonably sure Elissa was right, even if she, Fallon, didn't want her to be.

"She's not being critical," Kayla said. She moved forward and knelt in front of them. "It's true. You're real bossy about stuff, but we needed that. When our folks split up and Mom started looking to get married again, there wasn't anyone to take care of us. So you filled in the gap."

Fallon had known that she was the leader, but she'd never stopped to consider why. "I've always wanted to control things," she admitted. "In my heart, I guess it was about wanting to make everything a certain way because if it was right, I didn't have to be afraid."

Elissa nodded. "Just because we get older, it doesn't mean we change those rules. Even if the world is different, I don't think we allow ourselves to notice."

"You're right," Fallon said slowly as her sister's words sank in. "I know in my head that everything is different, but in my heart I'm still scared because my dad is gone and my mother doesn't notice me anymore."

"That was the worst," Kayla said, sadness replacing the usual humor in her green eyes. "She was so distant. It was as if we didn't exist."

Elissa nodded. "I thought nothing could be worse than the divorce, then Daddy died. Looking back, I wonder if they were ever in love."

"Does it matter?" Fallon asked. "Love does crazy things to people. I see it all the time at school. Parents split and the kids are the ones who suffer. I can always tell when there are problems at home. The children really act out. Love hurts.''

"You can't believe that," Elissa said gently. "Love can hurt, but it doesn't always.''

Fallon stared at her. "I know you and Cole are happy now, but there was a time when he broke your heart.''

Her sister flushed. "I broke his, too. We were too young. But we're grown and we've changed, and now we have a wonderful relationship. I don't want you to give up on love, Fallon. You need to let yourself experience it. I promise you'll never regret it.''

Fallon wasn't sure that was a promise she could believe.

"There were reasons Mom and Dad split up," Kayla said. "I'm sure we could guess at many of them, but the truth is, we were just kids and there were plenty of things we didn't know about them. You can't cut yourself off just because of the past. Elissa's right. You're a terrific woman, Fallon. You deserve an equally terrific guy in your life.''

"We were all afraid," Elissa added. "When Cole and I were first married, the fire between us burned so hot, it nearly burned out. We had to grow up enough to handle the responsibility. There are rewards in this, but you have to let go of the fear.''

"Easier said than done," Fallon grumbled. It was true. Loving someone like Anna Jane was easy and uncomplicated. Loving a man like Jarrett was something completely different. "I would want to love someone forever, but there are no guarantees. One thing I learned while working on the television show was how simple it is to make the illusion look real.''

"There is one guarantee," Elissa said.

Fallon glanced at her. "What's that?''

"If you don't risk loving someone, you'll always be alone."

"That's a cheerful thought." She didn't want to be alone. Losing her memory—thinking she had no one—had convinced her of that. But what were the alternatives? Taking a chance?

She wanted to tell them both that romantic love was just something that existed in people's imaginations. It wasn't real. Yet she knew it was. She'd seen it in her sisters' lives. She'd seen how love could transform two people. Most days she wanted that for herself. But the risk was so great.

"It's a lot of work," Kayla agreed. "But it's worth it. Loving Patrick is the best part of my life."

"What do you think of Jarrett?" Elissa asked Fallon.

"I don't know, and I mean that. I'm not sure of anything." Fallon shook her head. "This was so much easier when I was Ariel and didn't have a past. I could just feel, without having to think."

"You can still do that," Kayla said. "Don't let the fear win. I nearly lost Patrick because I was a fool. I'd hate to see the same thing happen to you. That's my advice, big sister. Be very, very sure before you walk away."

Fallon glanced from Kayla to Elissa. Both of them stared at her intently. She remembered their near disasters and knew they were right. "I'll be sure," she said, then wondered what she was agreeing to. She would rather have promised to look twice before leaping into love, but she had a nagging suspicion it was too late for that.

Anna Jane snuggled under the covers and smiled up at her uncle. He brushed her cheek with the backs of his fingers. "Happy?" he asked.

She nodded. "I had fun today." A yawn caught her off guard. She sighed sleepily. "I'm glad that Fallon and her sisters are here. And it's almost Christmas."

"I'm glad, too." Uncle Jarrett squeezed her fingers. "I want you to enjoy this time, honey."

"You want to know if I'm sad about Mommy and Nana B."

"Yes, I do."

She thought about what her life used to be like when she still lived in New York and nothing had changed. "This is different," she said. "Sometimes it's really nice being here."

"For a while I was afraid your mother had made a mistake leaving you with me," he admitted. "I've never had children before, so I don't always know what to say or how to act."

"You're doing a very nice job raising me."

He smiled. "Thank you. No matter what happens, or how I mess up, I want you to know that I'm grateful you're here. Your mother probably could have picked someone with more skills, but she couldn't have found someone who cares more than I do. You're a precious girl and I love you very much."

Anna Jane's chest got all tight as a funny feeling filled her tummy. She'd known her uncle cared, but she hadn't expected him to tell her. She sat up and flung her arms around him. "I love you, too, Uncle Jarrett."

He held her so close, she could feel his heart beating. The steady sound made her feel safe and warm. He was big and strong and he would look out for her. God had answered that prayer. Which only left the one about Uncle Jarrett and Fallon falling in love with each other. She snuggled closer to her uncle and smiled into his shoulder.

It was nearly Christmas, and everyone knew Christmas was a time for miracles.

Fallon tiptoed down the stairs. It was late and she should be asleep, but for some reason she felt restless. The past couple of days had been wonderful. She'd spent time with her sisters and their husbands. There had been long conversations, pool games, great food and general good times. Having Jarrett and Anna Jane as part of the group had only added to the fun. After all she'd been through today, she should be pleasantly exhausted. But she wasn't. Her mind wasn't willing to quiet enough to allow her to sleep. Maybe a quick stroll on the beach would help her unwind.

As she reached the main floor, she automatically glanced toward Jarrett's office. Instead of darkness, she saw the door closed and a light shining onto the marble floor. She frowned. What was he doing up this late?

Not sure if she would be intruding or not, she crossed the foyer and tapped on his door. Seconds later he flung it open and stared at her.

"What's wrong?" Fallon asked, taking in his rumpled clothing. His dark hair was ruffled as if he'd been running his fingers through it.

"You're awake," he said, his voice low with tension. "Thank God. I wanted to come and get you but I thought you'd already gone to bed."

Panic flared low in Fallon's stomach. "Is something wrong with Anna Jane?"

"What?" Jarrett grabbed her arm and pulled her into the room. "No, she's fine." He shook his head. "Dammit, I never expected this to be so difficult."

Alarm made her throat tighten. "Is someone ill?"

"Ill? What are you talking about? I need help with that."

He pointed. She glanced in that direction and saw piles of boxes littering his desk. An empty card table had been set up in the center of the room. On the floor were rolls of wrapping paper and ribbon. Bows were everywhere. Some of her concern faded.

"What are you doing?" she asked.

"Trying to wrap presents. It's about the hardest thing I've ever had to do. How do you manage it? There are all these different-size boxes. What ribbon goes with what paper? And what in God's name are you supposed to write on these stupid little cards?"

He grabbed a sheet of gift tags and tossed them into the air. "There's too much room for just names, but not enough room for a proper message. Besides, after the third or fourth present, it's tough to be creative."

Fallon felt a giggle forming in the back of her throat. She swallowed the sound. The relief was sweet, as was Jarrett's confusion. "Are you telling me you can save an empire but you can't figure out how to wrap a few presents?"

He glared at her. "I'm not in a good mood, Fallon. This isn't the time to make fun of me."

She wrinkled her nose. "It's exactly the time. If I don't take advantage of your weakened condition, I may never get this opportunity again." She looked at the mess he'd made of the single wrapped box on the chair by the window.

"How long have you been working on this?" she asked.

"Two hours."

Laughter bubbled again. This time she wasn't able to stifle the sound. He glared at her.

"May I remind you that I'm your host and as the guest, you owe me courtesy?"

"Jarrett, you're one swell guy and I'm being very courteous. It's just that wrapping packages is so easy. I can't believe you're this inept."

His dark eyebrows drew together. "Inept?"

"What else would you call it?"

He thought for a second. "A lack of field experience."

"Uh-huh. Do you want my help?"

He sagged with relief. "Yes. Please."

"No problem. I wrap a pretty terrific package, if I do say so myself." She glanced around the room. "The first thing we have to do is get organized."

She had him collect all the supplies. Then she sorted packages by size. There was a huge box, which was obviously a computer for Anna Jane. In fact, everything he'd bought the child was what she, Fallon, had recommended. There were a few things for Leona and Frank, plus gifts for her family.

She fingered the beautiful leather-bound photo album he'd bought Elissa and Cole. "You didn't have to do this," she said, grateful she'd already ordered Jarrett several presents. At least she didn't have to worry about her family facing him empty-handed on Christmas morning. "As you just reminded me, we're *your* guests here. Allowing us to stay is enough of a gift."

He shrugged. "I wanted to give them something. Anna Jane is very happy to have you here, and so am I."

His confession warmed her from the inside out. To cover her sudden shyness, she pointed to a large roll of paper. "See if that will fit around the computer box," she said. "If it doesn't, we'll have to patch a couple of pieces together."

While he did as she requested, she went to work on

several packages of software. "Anna Jane seems to be having fun," Fallon said. "She's spent the past couple of days laughing a lot."

"I agree." He unrolled the paper and stretched it out in the center of the floor, anchoring the edges with scissors and a roll of tape. "You're a teacher, right?"

"Fifth graders."

"What should I do with her? A few days ago you and I talked about several options—none of which I liked. She has to go to school, and there isn't one on the island."

"There also aren't any children, Jarrett. Being around here is fine for now, but she is going to need kids her own age to play with."

"Yeah. I've been thinking about that. You're the expert. What should I do?"

"What do you want to do?"

The paper just fit around the box. He tapped it in place, then carefully folded the two sides down. "I could bring in a tutor. While that gets her an education, it doesn't deal with the lack of children her age. There are a couple of good schools on nearby islands. She could board there during the week and come back on weekends. Or she could board in the States and come here during long breaks."

She unrolled ribbon and wrapped it around the dancing-reindeer-covered software boxes. "How do you feel about those?"

"I don't like them. I can't believe I'm going to say this, but I would miss her if she were gone. Given the choice, I want us to be together."

"But?"

"Yeah, but. But she needs more than me in her life. I

have to decide based on what's best for her, not what's easiest or most comfortable for me."

His willingness to sacrifice touched her. She'd known from the beginning that Jarrett was a special man. How was she supposed to resist someone who obviously cared so much about his niece?

"I'm a little concerned about boarding school in any form," he continued. "I remember what you told me she said about losing her mother and Nana B. I don't want her to think that she's being abandoned again."

"You could tell her the options and let her pick," Fallon said. "Going away might not be so scary then."

"I hadn't thought of that." He finished wrapping the computer and grinned in triumph. "Well?"

The paper didn't quite meet on one side and the pattern was crooked, but Fallon knew Anna Jane wouldn't care. "It's beautiful. Want to put a bow on it?"

He nodded and sorted through the selection. The large floppy bow he chose didn't match at all, but again Fallon didn't say anything. This was one time when the thought was definitely what mattered most.

She picked up another box, this one containing a beautiful blouse for Leona. "There is another option," she said, wondering if he would be angry with her for mentioning it.

"What's that?"

She drew in a deep breath and looked at him. "You could move back to the States. That way Anna Jane would be able to attend a regular school during the day and come home to you at night."

Her words hung in the silent room. Several emotions flashed through his eyes, but she couldn't identify any of them. He'd discussed his past with her; she knew what she was asking. That he give up the safety of the island and return to the world.

"I know what I'm saying," she told him, her voice soft. "I remember what you've been through. While I can't imagine all you've suffered, I have an idea about it. But this isn't about you, it's about your niece. I'm not telling you it's the only thing that would work, I'm just pointing out that it's worth considering."

She braced herself for the explosion. Jarrett bent over, picked up the computer and carried it out of the room. She went back to her wrapping, not sure if he was going to reappear. A minute later he walked into the room.

"Moving back is an option," he said at last. "You're right. It's something I have to consider. I can't stay here forever and I can't keep her isolated."

Jarrett glanced around the room. "Last year at this time, I was hard at work. I'm not sure I even noticed which day was Christmas. I gave Leona and Frank a big check and the week off. Someone from the hotel brought me meals." He shoved his hands into his jeans pockets. "Everything has changed. One day I got the call about my sister, three days later, after the funeral, Anna Jane was here. I didn't know what to do with her, and if there'd been a way to send her away, I would have. Now I can't imagine what it would be like without her. I think I would miss her very much."

"You love her."

He nodded. "I do."

He was, she realized, the best kind of man. Honorable, caring. No wonder her heart was at risk every time they were together.

She remembered what her sisters had said about taking a chance on romantic love. Their lives had worked out, but would hers? She'd always assumed she would spend her life alone. Until she'd met Jarrett, she'd been content with that fate. Now she wasn't. Now she wanted more. She wanted him.

At the thought, she became hyperaware of his body, of the quiet of the night, of how alone they were. A shiver raced through her. How she wished he would walk over to her and take her in his arms. She wanted to feel him press against her. She wanted to taste him again, to have his kisses drive her to madness.

"So you're the organized one," he said, his words breaking her mood.

She glanced down at the package she was wrapping and was pleased to see she hadn't mangled it completely. She smoothed the paper and secured it in place with a small piece of tape.

"That's me. The oldest by at least a couple of minutes and the bossy one."

"So you're used to getting your way, too?"

She smiled. "Always."

"I'm surprised we work so well together. What with us both being bossy."

She picked out a bow. "We're a good team because we respect each other's abilities."

He cleared packages off his chair and sat down. "I don't think so."

"You don't respect my abilities?"

"Of course I do, but that's not the point. You can be as bossy as you want, Fallon. We both know I could take you."

She blinked. "Are you saying you're in charge simply because you're physically stronger?"

His grin turned wicked. "Uh-huh."

"That's insane."

"Maybe, but it's true."

She placed her hands on her hips. "With an attitude like that, I'm not sure I should help you."

He looked at the few packages remaining. "You don't have to, anyway. I can finish up." He rose to his feet and approached her. Humor still lurked in his eyes, but it was tempered with a fire that made her breathing suddenly speed up.

"Thank you," he said.

"Um, you're welcome." Her palms got sweaty and she rubbed them together.

He stared at her for several heartbeats. "It's been a long time since I've wanted a woman." His voice was low and husky. "I'd nearly forgotten how good that could feel."

Before she could answer, he brushed his mouth against hers. The contact seared her down to her tingling toes. Then, as unexpectedly, he pulled back.

"I'm not going to walk you upstairs," he said calmly, as if discussing the weather. "It would be the polite thing to do, but I couldn't leave you at the door. Thank you for that, too, Fallon."

"I, ah..." She didn't know what to say. Had he just told her what she thought he'd told her? That he wanted her? Happiness made her giddy. She wanted to tell him that it was fine. She wanted him, too. In fact, if they both wanted each other so much, maybe they should do something about it. But while it was easy to be brave when talking about Anna Jane, it was quite another thing to be brave for herself. So instead of inviting him to her bed, or even kissing him back, she stumbled to the door and softly called good-night.

Chapter Thirteen

"**Y**ou have *not* seen flying reindeer," Anna Jane said firmly.

Cole, Elissa's husband, looked hurt. "Of course I have. Our apartment in New York is up very high. On Christmas Eve you can stand outside and watch Santa fly by. You can see the red glow in the sky from Rudolph's nose."

Anna Jane rolled her eyes. "I'm nine years old. I don't believe in Santa anymore."

Patrick winced. "Jeez, I hate it when kids say that. I'm a lot older than you and I still believe in Santa."

"You do not."

Patrick made an *X* in the center of his chest. "I sure do. I write a list every year and send it to the North Pole."

Kayla giggled. "He uses express mail and a signed receipt, just to make sure it really gets there."

"But you're a grown-up."

"Only on the outside," Kayla said, then laughed harder when her husband glared at her.

Patrick deliberately turned his back on his wife and looked at Anna Jane. "Sometimes you have to take a few things on faith, even if there's no proof."

Jarrett watched his niece wrestle with that piece of information. He knew she considered herself very mature for her age, and believing in Santa went against her definition of being grown-up. But she liked Patrick and Cole a lot.

"It's like love," Elissa said. "You can't see it or touch it, but you know it exists."

"Maybe." Anna Jane sounded doubtful. She turned to Fallon.

"Do you believe in Santa?"

"I believe in miracles, so that's almost the same thing." She held out her arms. Anna Jane moved next to her and leaned against Fallon.

At first Jarrett didn't recognize the source of the warmth spreading through him. Although he was sitting on the sofa relatively near Fallon, it wasn't just sexual desire. There was something else—and then he figured it out. Contentment.

He'd spent so much of his life alone—some by choice, some by necessity. He'd forgotten what it was like to be around good people, sharing good times. He'd grown used to solitary holidays and the silence. Tracy had invited him to visit her every Christmas, from the time she'd moved out and married Donald through last year. He'd always refused. Now, looking around the room, at the beautiful tree, the presents piled high, and listening to the happy conversation, he knew he'd been wrong to avoid the family connection. It was too late to change the past, but he made a vow it wasn't going to happen in the future.

"There are a lot of presents," Anna Jane said conversationally, sliding onto Fallon's lap and giving Jarrett an innocent look. Her dark eyes glittered with excitement. "So many presents. We'll be opening them for hours tomorrow."

He hid a smile. "It will be a lot of work," he agreed solemnly.

Fallon squeezed her tight. "I know what you're trying to do, and it's not going to work."

Anna Jane blinked several times. "I'm not doing anything."

"Uh-huh. Sure. You want to open presents tonight."

"I never said that, but it *is* a good idea, don't you think?"

Fallon laughed.

Jarrett couldn't have found the strength to look away, even if he'd wanted to. There was something so compelling about watching Fallon with Anna Jane. It was as if the two of them were family, instead of a woman and child who had just met. He suspected some of the connection had been born from their mutual needs. Anna Jane had recently lost every important person in her world. As Ariel, Fallon had lost her identity. Those losses had allowed them to form a bond that was stronger than casual acquaintance.

But while he could explain away Fallon's relationship with his niece, he didn't have such an easy explanation for his attraction to the woman who had recently become an important part of his world.

Last night he'd admitted to her that he wanted her. He was still surprised by that. Not the feelings; he'd resisted desire from the first moment he'd seen her. Instead, he was startled that he'd willingly told her how he felt. It had been years since he'd allowed himself to physically crave anyone. Longer still since he'd trusted a single soul with personal information. What was it about her that made him want to risk caring?

"Jarrett, you're going to have to make the decision," Fallon said, breaking in to his thoughts. "Anna Jane wants to open just one present."

"What's the tradition in your family?" he asked.

The triplets shared a quick look. "There wasn't one," Kayla said quickly. "Some years we were allowed to open presents on Christmas Eve and some years we had to wait. What about you, Patrick?"

"I'm a sucker for big brown eyes," Patrick said easily. "I doubt I could refuse Anna Jane anything."

"I like Patrick," the girl declared.

"I'll bet you do," Jarrett told her. "All right. One present. But I get to pick which one."

Fallon looked at him. "Why do I get the feeling I don't know about this?"

"Because you don't. I did some of the wrapping myself."

Anna Jane jumped to the ground and clapped her hands together. "Yes! I like this tradition. Which package?"

Elissa glanced at Fallon. "Are you thinking what I'm thinking?"

"Unfortunately, yes. Jarrett, you didn't, did you?"

"Did what?" Anna Jane asked.

Kayla groaned and pulled her knees up to her chest. "Oh, Lord, I can't stand this. I really hope we're wrong."

Jarrett walked over to the tree and dug around in the wrapped packages until he found the right one. The rectangular box was about the size of half a loaf of bread.

"It's not," Kayla said. "The size is wrong."

"Unless it's a set," Fallon muttered darkly.

"I'm going to open it," Anna Jane told them. "Then we'll know."

Jarrett stood next to his niece and grinned in anticipation. The triplets were right, and he couldn't wait to see the look on Fallon's face.

Anna Jane ripped at the brightly colored wrapping paper. It fluttered to the floor. She stared at the boxed set of six videos. She frowned as she stared at the photograph on the jacket. "'The Sally McGuire Show,'" she read aloud. "Why would—" Her expression cleared. "Oh, Uncle Jarrett, this is Fallon's show. You bought me Fallon's show!"

Fallon fell over on the sofa and covered her face with her hands. "I can't believe he found them."

"Worse," Elissa said. "Think about where we are. He not only found them, he had them flown in specially."

"I, for one, am pleased," Cole told his wife. "I like watching the show."

"That's because you weren't in it," Fallon muttered, still huddled on the sofa. "You didn't have your humiliation recorded and then sold in a boxed gift set." "I'm with Cole," Patrick said. "The videos are great. Where's the television?"

Fallon made a whimpering sound. "Please don't make us watch them on the big-screen TV upstairs."

Jarrett tried to look apologetic, even though he didn't feel it in the least. "Sorry, that's the only one in the house."

"You have a set in your office," Fallon reminded him.

"It's very small and it only gets CNN."

She raised her head. "Liar."

He winked. "I'm excited about this."

"Me, too," Anna Jane said, and raced for the door. "I'll go and turn on the TV."

Patrick got to his feet and held out his hand to his wife. Kayla moaned. "But I don't want to have to watch these."

"Quit whining. It'll be fun."

She shook her head, but obligingly let him pull her into a standing position. Cole was already leading Elissa out the door and toward the stairs.

Jarrett looked at Fallon. "It can't be that awful."

She raised her head, then blew her bangs off her forehead. "See, that's where you're wrong. It *is* that awful. I love my sisters and they love me, but that doesn't change the fact that none of us were very good actors. We managed to get by with a lot of takes and help. Despite our mother's urging, we were not destined for this as a career."

"What's your point?"

"I don't have one. I'm just whining."

"Whine upstairs."

The media room had three overstuffed leather sofas all facing a huge television. Anna Jane bounced from foot to foot as the adults found seats.

"I've already put the tape in," she announced.

Jarrett winked at her. "I'm glad you're not impatient or anything."

"I'm not," she declared. "You guys are taking too long."

"Just start it," Fallon said as she collapsed onto the sofa on the left. "It's not as if we haven't seen these before."

Jarrett was pleased when she half turned toward him,

tucking one foot under her and leaning her head against the sofa.

"I promise not to laugh," he told her.

"Yeah, but will you still respect me?"

Something flickered in her green eyes. Something that made him think about last night, when he'd told her he wanted her and had seen a delighted light in her eyes...right before she'd blushed.

"I'll always respect you," he answered. They weren't still talking about the show, and he suspected she knew that.

"Okay, I'm gonna start it now," Anna Jane announced, and hit a button on the remote control. The blue screen flickered once, then was filled with the FCC warning about making copies.

"This is fun," she said, and headed for the small space between him and Fallon.

As she cuddled next to him, Jarrett waited to feel annoyed at the intrusion. Oddly, he didn't. While he would have liked to have had Fallon in his arms, she was close enough. Right now Anna Jane needed him more. He was determined to do right by her.

"I picked the Christmas story," Anna Jane said. "It's about a baby left on the doorstep."

Elissa laughed delightedly. "It's my favorite episode," she told Anna Jane.

Across the room Kayla stuck out her tongue. "Figures."

Fallon glanced at him. "Elissa was sick that week," she explained. "I don't think she has a single scene in this entire show. It was just Kayla and me, acting badly." She shook her head. "Hmm, that didn't come out right. Badly acting? Is that better?"

The credits ended and the show began. A baby sat in

a basket on a doorstep. Fake snow lined the cobblestone street.

A blond, curly-headed young girl came around the side of the building and spotted the infant. Green eyes widened in shock. "Oh, look!" she said loudly. "Someone left a baby on the doorstep."

Kayla and Elissa burst out laughing. Fallon covered her face with her hands. "I don't want to watch this."

Jarrett looked from the child on the screen to her. "That's you?"

Still hiding her head, she nodded. "Yup. Can't you see that natural ability shining through?"

"I like it," Anna Jane said.

"Thanks, sweetie. At least the story is fun."

Jarrett found it odd to look at a preteen on the television screen and absorb the fact that the grown-up version was sitting next to him on his sofa. When Kayla played Sally, Patrick was quick to point out there'd been a change in actors. Jarrett studied Fallon's sister and realized there were small but significant differences between them, even then.

The story line followed the attempts of the children to keep the baby hidden for fear it was too young and would be sent away. Eventually they were found out, and at the end of the show the baby was adopted.

The last scene showed all the orphan children singing in front of the Christmas tree, while a smiling young couple held their new child.

Anna Jane sat up straight. "I don't think I want to go live in an orphanage."

Fallon put her arm around the girl. "Honey, that's just pretend. None of those children really lived in an orphanage. They were acting, like my sisters and me."

"But some children live there."

"Some, but not many. You don't."

"Hey, don't worry," Jarrett said, squeezing her hand. "You've got me. I'll take care of you."

Big brown eyes widened. "You promise you won't send me there? Even if I'm really, really bad?"

"I promise. I couldn't do that, Anna Jane. I'd miss you too much."

She seemed to weigh his words, then she nodded as if she'd made a decision. "I'd miss you, too," she announced, then pushed off the sofa. "I want to watch another one."

"I know what you're thinking," Fallon said softly. "Don't worry. You're doing a great job with her."

"I wish I could be as sure."

"I'm the expert," she reminded him. "I see parents with kids all the time. Trust me. You guys are going to do well together. Probably right up until she wants to get her driver's license."

"Don't remind me."

He looked at the young girl changing the video. She moved with a lightness and grace that reminded him of his sister. He hadn't wanted her around, but now that she was here, he couldn't imagine life without her. So where did that leave him? She needed friends and schooling; he didn't want to leave the island. He doubted she would want to consider boarding school, and he wasn't all that fond of the idea, either. So what were the options? Fallon had reminded him he could always move back to the States.

He stiffened, trying to ignore old memories and pain. Yet he wasn't sure he had a choice. He would have to do what was best for the child and let the past take care of itself.

* * *

The logs in the fireplace had been reduced to ash. Elissa stared at them. "It's getting late," she said, but made no move to stand.

Fallon glanced at the beautiful grandfather clock in the corner. "Nearly midnight."

Elissa smiled and squeezed her arm. "Happy Christmas, Fallon. We're glad to have you back."

"I'm glad to be back." She sipped her brandy, then swirled the glass. "All those months ago when we made our plans for a tropical Christmas, who would have thought we would end up here?"

"I know." Elissa leaned back on the living-room sofa. "Where was it? At Kayla's?"

"Yes. For our twenty-fifth birthday. Now it's barely six months later. You're back with Cole, Kayla's married to Patrick and there's already a baby on the way."

"And what about you?" Elissa asked.

Fallon looked across the room to where Cole and Jarrett were talking business. Kayla and Patrick had already gone up to bed, as had an excited Anna Jane.

"I'm putting my life back together," Fallon said. "In another couple of days I'm sure I will have sorted everything out."

"Does that everything include Jarrett?"

Fallon thought about the question. "I had feelings for him when I was Ariel, but I didn't know if I was married or involved or what."

"Now you know you're single."

"That's true."

"Have the feelings changed?"

"No. Not at all. I like him." She stared at his chiseled profile. "He's gorgeous and kind and smart and funny. What's not to like?"

"But?"

Fallon raised her eyebrows. "You're grilling me."

"Very gently. Kayla and I are curious. Do you blame us?"

"No. I just want to be sure."

Elissa set her drink on the coffee table. "Sometimes you have to take a chance. Life isn't always a sure thing."

"Agreed. But for now, I'm just going to see what happens."

Elissa closed her eyes. "Kayla wants to know if we're going to call Mom tomorrow."

Fallon's good mood dampened slightly. "Sure. We'll wish her Merry Christmas, she'll tell us about the twins for fifteen minutes, then hang up."

"It's as if we don't exist for her anymore."

Fallon grimaced. "We stopped being show-business children. That was her dream and we stood in the way of that. I'm glad the twins are in movies, if that's what makes them happy. I've been over this in my mind and I think the trick is not to take it personally."

Elissa raised her eyebrows. "Hard to do when it's your own mother."

"At least we know we'll do better."

Cole and Jarrett rose to their feet. "You two are looking solemn," Cole said. "It's Christmas Eve and nothing sad is allowed."

"Yes, sir." Elissa smiled as she stood. Her husband wrapped his arms around her. "Night," she said. "See you in the morning."

"Good night," Fallon and Jarrett called after them.

Fallon swirled the bit of brandy still in the bottom of her glass. "I should head upstairs, too," she said, but made no move to stand. Jarrett walked to the sofa and sat next to her.

Except for the occasional faint snap from the fireplace, the room was quiet. A pleasant lethargy stole over her, draining her of free will. She would be content to stay here forever.

"What are you thinking?" Jarrett asked.

She leaned back, shifting so she faced him. A perfect male profile, she thought, her fingers itching to touch his face and the stubble darkening his jaw. "That this Christmas is turning out to be pretty wonderful," she replied. "If a little strange."

He angled toward her and their knees bumped. His jeans brushed against the flowing silk of her green skirt. "What's strange about it?"

She smiled slowly. "The windows are open and I can hear the ocean. Twenty minutes ago there was a fire burning brightly. It's an odd combination."

"Do you miss snow?"

"No. There wasn't any in Los Angeles. Well, maybe once every twelve years or something, but never on Christmas."

"At least we don't have the air-conditioning on. That's happened a few years."

"How many holiday seasons have you spent here?"

He shrugged. "Five or six."

"Alone?"

"Sure."

She thought about her own family. While she and her sisters weren't close with their mother anymore, and their father had died many years ago, at least they had each other.

"Does that bother you?" she asked.

"It didn't," he said. "Now that I've experienced how the other half lives, I'm not sure I could go back. Earlier I was thinking about all the invitations Tracy issued to me. Maybe I shouldn't have refused them. I would have liked to spend time with her and her family.''

''You have Anna Jane now,'' she reminded him. ''She's wonderful, and she's going to make all your holidays special.''

''What about your parents?'' he asked.

''Elissa and I were just talking about that. I wish that…'' Her voice trailed off. ''It's weird. When we were growing up and our folks were still together, I thought it would always be like that. They fought a lot, but I figured everyone's mom and dad fought. Then they split up and a few years later our dad died. Nothing has ever been the same.''

''Your mother remarried?''

''Almost right after the divorce. She was very disappointed when my sisters and I refused to continue to be in 'show' business.'' She said the word bitterly. ''Now she has twins and they're working steadily. It's what she always wanted.''

''But you're not close.''

''No.'' She frowned, remembering the past. ''It's almost as if my parents bought into the myth of television, of the perfect family with perfect children. When that didn't turn out to be real, they didn't want any part of it. That attitude is one of the reasons I went into teaching. Kids are completely genuine.''

''I'm surprised you don't have a couple dozen of your own.''

''I'd like to.''

She would. But in her mind, children meant family and that implied a husband and father. So far there hadn't been anyone she was comfortable thinking of that way. Except for Jarrett. As she had been when she'd read her journal a couple of days ago, she was struck by how solitary her plans for the future had been.

"How do you survive being alone?" she asked. "I hadn't realized that was what I expected for myself until recently, but apparently it's the truth. I don't like it and I'm not sure how to change it."

He looked at her. Sadness darkened his eyes to the color of midnight. "I wouldn't wish it on a snake," he said. "It's not living, it's existing. You deserve more, Fallon. Don't give up so easily."

"I don't want to, it's just—"

How could she tell him there had never been anyone around to make her think otherwise?

"You have your sisters," he reminded her.

"That's not exactly the relationship I had in mind."

She hadn't noticed him moving, but suddenly he seemed to be sitting closer. She inhaled and caught his scent—an intriguing combination of male and cologne. A shiver rippled down her spine.

"What *do* you want?" he asked softly.

She didn't know how to answer. She wasn't sure what he was asking. Still, the word fell past her lips with no conscious thought on her part. "More."

With one fluid, masterful gesture, he swept her into his arms. She went willingly, surging toward him, wrapping one arm around his neck, plunging her fingers through his hair. As his mouth came down to hers, she was ready, her lips already parted.

Jarrett resisted the powerful impulse to plunge into her mouth. As much as he wanted her, he knew it would be better if he held himself in check and savored the kiss. So he drew back at the last second and swept his tongue across her lower lip. She shuddered and whispered his name. The hand gripping his shoulder tightened. Her legs shifted restlessly as if she, too, felt uncontrollable hunger.

He cupped her head, burying his fingers in her loose curls. The soft silk of her hair caressed him. When he had teasingly circled her mouth, he slowly slipped inside, first laying claim to the sensitive skin of her inner lip before touching his tongue to the tip of hers.

Fire engulfed him. The need was incendiary, inescapable and instantaneous. His arousal throbbed with his rapid heartbeat. Every square inch of his body longed to be naked and pressed intimately against her. As he tilted his head and swept in deeper, he dropped one hand to her shoulder, then down her arm.

At the base of her elbow he slipped to her ribs. She clamped her lips around his tongue and sucked on him. The unexpected assault left him breathless and ready. He gave a guttural groan and cupped her breast.

The sweet curve nestled in his palm. His fingers curled around her as his thumb brushed over her taut nipple. The sucking increased, then stopped. She tilted her head back, gasping for air. He could see the rapid pulse at the base of her throat, and when she opened her eyes to look at him, desire clouded her green irises. Her mouth was swollen from their kisses.

"Jarrett, I—"

"Yeah," he whispered, releasing her breast and pulling her hard against him. "Me, too."

He kissed her cheek, her forehead, her nose and finally her mouth. When she parted her lips, he moved in slowly, sensuously, savoring the taste, the texture, all of her.

He was hard and hot and he suspected if he touched her between her silken thighs he would find her already wet. She obviously wanted him as much as he wanted her. Which made his decision not to make love tonight completely crazy.

If asked, he wouldn't be able to explain it. Yet some voice in his head warned this wasn't the right time. He knew down to his heart that making love with Fallon would be completely different from making love with anyone else. She had already invaded his life; he wasn't ready to have her invade his soul.

He pulled back and smiled. "It's late," he said. "We should both be in bed."

Her eyes widened.

"Separate beds," he explained.

Questions swept across her face. Questions he couldn't answer. He wasn't sure why he was holding back. Maybe it was a mistake, but he didn't think so.

The grandfather clock chimed the hour, and the melodious sound of bells interrupted his thoughts. They both glanced at the face of the clock. It was midnight.

"Merry Christmas," he told her.

She stood, then bent at the waist and softly kissed his mouth. "Merry Christmas, Jarrett. And thank you."

Chapter Fourteen

"You have to smile, Uncle Jarrett," Anna Jane said.

Jarrett glanced up and smiled obligingly. The nine-year-old raised her new disposable camera to her right eye and pushed the button. When the picture was taken, she grinned. "This is fun."

He had to agree. The living room looked as if there'd been a whirlwind through the place. Wrapping paper, empty boxes, bows and tags were scattered all around. Piles of presents teetered in different corners of the room. Again he was reminded of how things could have been if he'd allowed himself to accept his sister's invitations. Yet he'd deliberately withdrawn. Had it been a form of punishment?

The thought hadn't occurred to him before, but now that he mulled it over, it made sense. Despite the fact that he had tried to make things right with Charlotte and that he'd never wanted anything to happen to her, he still blamed himself for her death. A voice in his head kept telling him he should have known she was unstable before he ever started their affair. There hadn't been any outward clues, but he was supposed to be good with people. Why hadn't he sensed it?

All the logic in the world didn't matter when guilt was involved. She'd died and he was responsible. She'd been buried in the ground, he'd buried himself alive, drowning in work, refusing to participate in the pleasures of life. Until one small girl and an amazing woman had returned him to the land of the living.

He wanted to go back in time and make it right with Charlotte and with Tracy. He wanted to relive those first years of Anna Jane's life and watch her grow into the terrific kid she was today. But that wasn't possible. He wasn't going to get a chance to change the past, but he had been given another opportunity with the future.

"You're looking happy about something," Fallon said.

She sat cross-legged on the floor next to him. It had dawned clear and warm for Christmas and they were all in shorts. Fallon wore her hair loose, the way he liked it best. Minimal makeup accentuated her large eyes and tempting mouth. Now, as she smiled at him, all he could think about was stealing her away from the family scene and kissing her until they forgot everything except how much they wanted each other.

"I finally get the point of Dickens's story *A Christmas Carol*," he said. "I know exactly how Ebenezer Scrooge felt that morning."

"Don't tell me you've been seeing ghosts," she teased.

"Not exactly, but I have come to my senses."

"I'm glad."

"You're partially responsible."

A faint blush stained her cheeks. "That's not true, Jarrett. You managed this all on your own. I was just the catalyst. If I hadn't shown up, you would have figured out what to do."

"Not in time to give Anna Jane a nice holiday."

"You underestimate yourself."

He wished she were telling the truth, but he knew better. He would have continued to bury himself in his work, because it was easier than learning how to deal with a child. He shuddered at the thought of Anna Jane's disappointment. Thank God Fallon had helped him avert that crisis.

Kayla said something, capturing Fallon's attention. Jarrett looked at the happy couples in the room. They nearly glowed with their affection for each other. He envied them that. Love between a man and a woman still terrified him. He knew the cost of loving someone to the exclusion of all else. It was safer to be alone. And yet— He drew in a breath. Being around Fallon made him want more. And wanting more was the reason he hadn't made love to her last night.

He smiled at the thought. If he hadn't wanted her so much, he would have taken her to his bed. If she hadn't been starting to get under his skin it would have been easy to find comfort and release in her beautiful body. But his confused feelings complicated the situation. For now it was easier to hold back.

Anna Jane flopped down in front of him. "This has been a wonderful Christmas, Uncle Jarrett. Thank you very much."

He looked at her and frowned. "There are two more packages."

Her dark eyes widened as a slow grin split her face. "Really?"

"Yes. One for you and one for Fallon. I'm surprised you missed them."

Anna Jane got up and walked over to the tree. The area underneath was empty. "There's nothing here."

"Check the lower branches. When I ran out of room on the floor, I put a couple of things there."

"Oh, here they are," she squealed as she handed her camera to Cole and reached for the packages. One was a three-inch-square box, the other a flat box about six by eight inches. Anna Jane read the tags and handed the larger gift to Fallon. "They're from Uncle Jarrett," she said.

Fallon raised her eyebrows. She pointed to the impressive pile in front of her. There were a couple of books, a T-shirt from the resort, some perfume and a large box of imported chocolates. "You've already done more than enough."

He shrugged. "This is different." He turned his attention to his niece. "You have to open yours first, Anna Jane."

The child ripped off the paper and lifted the cover from the box. She exhaled a sigh of pure pleasure as she pulled out a delicate chain with a pendant. "It's beautiful," she said, her voice laced with awe. "Uncle Jarrett, it's the most beautiful thing I've ever, ever seen."

She laid the pendant in her hand and held it out to him. The jeweler had worked a miracle, and in record time. As Jarrett had requested, the pendant was a small golden mermaid with a pretty smile and long curly hair. She wore a crown of tiny pearls. Her arms were outstretched as if she were offering a gift. Her miniature fingers clutched a twenty-five-point diamond.

Fallon felt her throat tighten as she stared at the pendant. Just when she figured Jarrett had gotten as close as he could to stealing her heart, he went and did something like this. The warm, thoughtful gesture warned her she was in more danger than she'd first realized.

"It's amazing," she said.

Her sisters crowded around. "Stunning," Elissa agreed. "But why a mermaid?"

"When I couldn't remember my name, Anna Jane called me Ariel, after the mermaid in the Disney movie. Because I'd washed up on the beach."

"Oh, that's so sweet," Kayla said. "Between Christmas and my wayward hormones, I just might have to cry."

Anna Jane held the necklace out to Jarrett, then stood with her back to him and lifted her hair off her neck. "Put it on me, Uncle Jarrett. I want to wear it."

He did as she requested. When the necklace was secure, Anna Jane spun around and threw herself at him. She wrapped her arms around him and held on tightly. "I love it and I love you."

"Brat," he said affectionately. "I'm glad."

Still in his embrace, Anna Jane looked at Fallon. "Open yours."

Fallon had an idea she was about to receive a grown-up version of the girl's necklace and she could already feel tears burning in her eyes.

"I refuse to cry," she muttered.

"Oh, happy tears, Uncle Jarrett. That's good, huh?"

"I hope so," he replied.

Fallon didn't dare look at him or her sisters. She tugged at the wrapping paper, then let it fall to the floor. The flat jeweler's box was pale, salmon-colored velvet. Emotionally bracing herself, she opened the top.

Her breath caught in her throat. Instead of a pendant,

she stared down at a strand of perfectly matched pearls. They were smooth and gleaming in the morning light.

"Oh, my," she breathed. She didn't think she'd ever seen anything so lovely.

Kayla and Elissa crowded close. "Boy howdy, there's a present," Kayla said, and grinned. "I can hardly wait to borrow them."

Fallon smiled slightly, then sobered. "Jarrett, these are too expensive. I can't accept."

Elissa and Kayla both groaned. "Are you insane?" Kayla asked.

"I—"

"He wants you to have them," Elissa added. "Right, Jarrett?"

"Of course. Otherwise I wouldn't have bought them."

Fallon risked a quick glance. Jarrett was smiling at her. "It's okay," he said in a mock whisper. "I can afford them."

Anna Jane leaned over her shoulder. "They're nice, Uncle Jarrett, but I thought there would be a mermaid."

"There is." He pointed to the tissue-wrapped object in the center of the box.

Fallon felt her fingers start to shake. She rested the box on the floor and picked up the small package. It felt heavy. As she unwrapped it, she felt the shape of the mermaid's tail. When she finally held the golden beauty in her hand, she gasped.

The mermaid was a larger version of Anna Jane's. The only difference was there were no pearls in her mermaid's crown and the small diamond in her hands had been replaced with a much larger stone.

"So you can remember her," Jarrett said.

"Ariel or Anna Jane?" she asked.

"Both." He pointed to the solid gold object. "It's a

pearl enhancer. You can wear the strand with or without it. The mermaid will fit on a wide chain, too."

"I don't know what to say," she said, feeling numb. Something damp trickled down her cheek. She brushed at her chin and was shocked to realize she was crying.

Anna Jane leaned close. "Say 'thank you,'" the child whispered.

"I really shouldn't—"

"Fallon!" Kayla and Elissa said together.

"I—" She clamped her lips together and tried again. "Thank you."

Still holding the mermaid, she rose onto her knees and hugged him. As he squeezed her back she felt something tighten, then release in her chest. A warm glow filled her. Over Jarrett's shoulder she saw Kayla give her a thumbs-up sign.

Fallon laughed and fought tears and wondered if any moment in her life had ever been this perfect.

"This is crazy," Fallon said. "I refuse to cry. I'll see you guys in a few weeks."

Elissa hugged her close. "It won't be soon enough. This has been a great holiday."

She crouched down and hugged Anna Jane. The nine-year-old didn't attempt to hide her tears. They flowed freely.

"I'll miss you, little one," Elissa told her.

"I'll miss you, too. I wish you didn't have to go."

Jarrett placed his hand on his niece's shoulder. "They'll come back."

Kayla laughed. "You can bet on it." She stretched her T-shirt over her barely rounded belly. "The next time you see me, I'll be skinny and gorgeous again."

"You're already beautiful," Jarrett told her. "Pregnancy only enhances that."

"Hey, that's my line," Patrick said, and grinned.

Kayla laid the back of her hand across her forehead. "I swear I'm going to swoon. Keep this one, Fallon. There aren't enough like him out there."

Her sister was right, Fallon thought. She wasn't sure how, but she'd gotten lucky with Jarrett. He'd made the time with her family the best Christmas they'd ever had.

The sisters hugged while the men shook hands. Everyone took turns kissing Anna Jane on the cheek. She waved bravely as they climbed into the charter plane that would take them to Miami.

"Bye," Anna Jane called as the door closed.

Fallon waved as her family took their seats and waved back. In a matter of minutes, the plane had disappeared into the brilliant blue sky.

Jarrett bent and picked up Anna Jane. He put his arm around Fallon. "It's New Year's Eve tomorrow," he reminded them. "Are you two going to be down in the dumps for that?"

Anna Jane sniffed. "Are we having a party?"

"Of course. We're going to the hotel and they're having a big party."

Anna Jane smiled through her tears. "Can I stay up until midnight?"

"I don't know. Can you?"

She giggled. "*May* I stay up until midnight?"

"Yes, you may. If you can."

Fallon laughed with them. Like Anna Jane, she was sorry to see her sisters go, but the prospect of dancing the night away in Jarrett's arms tomorrow night had its own appeal. She'd bought a sexy dress from the boutique, just for the occasion. She wanted to impress him. And maybe knock him a little off balance. It was only fair; he did that to her every time he smiled at her.

The hotel ballroom had been decorated with balloons and streamers. Black, gold and silver moons and stars covered the tables and hung from slender strings. The hotel had flown the band in from the States and their combination of contemporary and jazz had everyone out on the dance floor. Anna Jane was a hit with all the young boys staying at the resort.

"She's having a wonderful time," Fallon said as Jarrett made a quick turn. She followed his steps, moving her body with his but keeping her attention on his niece.

"The belle of the ball."

"Lucky for her all the kids seem to be boys. Although I suspect she would be this popular even without those numbers in her favor."

She said the words without thinking. Jarrett would have bet his entire fortune on that fact. Fallon didn't weigh her conversation and try to get the most mileage out of it. She spoke her mind, regardless of what others might think. Even without trying, she still got it right the first time. Her obvious affection for his niece made him care about her more. He wanted her, he liked her, he respected her. It was a deadly combination.

The music ended. They stepped apart and clapped. Jarrett took her bare arm and led her back to the table. He knew several of the men in the room were watching them, wondering about his relationship with the stunning creature at his side. He allowed himself a small smile. They could look, but they wouldn't be touching any part of her tonight.

"What are you so happy about?" she asked.

"I was thinking how beautiful you are," he told her.

She blushed. "Thank you. It's the dress."

She motioned to the strapless, beaded gown she wore. It started at her breasts, leaving a fair amount of cleavage exposed, skimmed over her waist and rounded hips, before stopping about six inches above her knees. The glittering fabric was the exact color of her eyes. High heels made her already long legs look even longer. With her hair piled on top of her head and makeup highlighting her perfect features, she was more supermodel than real woman. Maybe there were people who would disagree and point to other guests as more beautiful or sophisticated. Jarrett didn't care. Fallon was all he could see— all he wanted to see.

Anna Jane was waiting for them at the table. She finished a glass of water and fanned herself. "Did you watch me? I'm dancing. I hated those lessons Nana B. made me take, but now I'm glad. I can do all the dances." She wrinkled her nose. "I don't have to kiss any of those boys, do I?"

Jarrett stiffened at the thought. "Not only don't you have to, you're not allowed to. You're only nine years old. What on earth—"

Fallon laid a hand on his forearm. "Uncle Jarrett, don't overreact to the question."

Her calm voice had the desired affect. He realized Anna Jane was looking apprehensive. He bent and kissed her cheek. "I'm the only boy you'll be kissing tonight."

She laughed. "You're not a boy. You're all grown up." Her voice dropped to a whisper. "But I'm glad. Bobby told me there was kissing at midnight." She made a gagging noise. "I didn't think I'd like it."

The waiter appeared with more champagne for the adults and sparkling soda water for Anna Jane. The band started up again and yet another youngster appeared to claim the little girl.

"It's crazy," Jarrett said, watching her go off with a boy. "How am I supposed to handle dating? Maybe I could send her to an all-girls school."

Fallon smiled at him. "It wouldn't help. She'll still discover boys when she's ready."

"What about when I'm ready? Shouldn't she have to wait until then?"

"You're never going to be ready. Besides, it could be worse."

"How?"

"You could have triplet daughters."

He groaned at the thought. "I couldn't handle that." He pulled her into his arms and they moved back onto the dance floor. "About that midnight kiss," he said.

"Yes?"

"Well, will you mind very much?"

He felt her shiver slightly, and his own body hardened in anticipation. "'Mind' isn't the word I'd use," she said, her voice low and husky. "I was thinking more of anticipate."

But it didn't turn out to be an issue. Anna Jane faded shortly after ten and it was barely eleven by the time they returned home and he carried her to bed. Fallon came with him and got the young girl out of her fancy party dress and into her nightie. Jarrett peeled back th̶ ̶̶̶rs.

"I could have left you at the party," he ̶̶̶ ̶̶ as he placed Anna Jane in bed. She stirr̶̶̶ rolled onto her side.

Fallon shook her head. "Why ̶̶̶̶ there without you? This is fine. ̶̶̶̶ but I'm also happy to be bac̶̶̶

"Thanks." He wonde̶̶̶

would have understood. Probably about as many as would have been pleased to have Anna Jane tagging along in the first place.

They turned off the light and stepped into the hallway. For the first time in a long time, Jarrett was unsure of what to do next. He didn't want to leave Fallon, but he didn't know that he had the right to expect her company any longer. She might be tired. Or sick of being with him.

"I have champagne downstairs," he said. "But if you're sleepy, you're welcome to go to bed."

She moved away from Anna Jane's door and paused by her own. "I'm not the least bit sleepy," she told him.

He tried not to notice the fire in her eyes. He suspected it was there without her consent. Probably just a reaction to the night, or the dancing, or the champagne they'd already tasted.

Or maybe it was something else entirely. Maybe she was reacting to him the way he was reacting to her. Maybe she felt the need, too. Maybe the desire had kept *her* awake until dawn, just as it had kept him tossing and turning.

"Hell," he muttered, and ran his fingers through his hair.

"What's wrong?"

"I'm trying to decide if I'm going to be a gentleman or not."

"I could help you decide, if you could explain the difference."

Her voice—the melodious tones tugged at him like a siren's call. He tried not to notice how much of her breasts were exposed by her dress, or think about what happen to the garment if he undid the zipper. The looked heavy. Would it fall to the ground and leave her exposed before him? What exactly was she wearing underneath?

"If I were acting like a gentleman, I would invite you downstairs for more champagne."

Her eyes turned smoky and her mouth parted. "If you weren't acting like a gentleman?"

"I would invite myself into your bedroom...and your bed."

She stared at him for several heartbeats. It took him a couple of seconds to figure out he was damned nervous about her reaction. He didn't think rejection would kill him, but it would certainly rip a few holes in his hide.

Instead of answering, she reached behind her and turned the knob. The door swung open, as if beckoning them into the darkness.

Anticipation tightened his throat. "Fallon?"

"The whole gentleman thing is highly overrated," she murmured.

Chapter Fifteen

Fallon couldn't believe she'd been so bold. Judging from the look on Jarrett's face, he didn't believe it, either. She consoled herself with the thought that if nothing else, he appeared very happy.

He cupped her cheek in his hand and kissed her gently. She felt the warm contact all the way down to her toes. His fingertips gently stroked her cheekbone while his tongue traced the seam of her mouth. She parted for him, her body already hot and ready for what he offered.

But instead of plunging inside, he licked her lower lip, then teased at the sensitive skin inside. He held her still, tilted his head and nibbled at the corner of her mouth. His teeth gently pressed against the sensitive skin. Her breath caught in her throat.

At the sound, he shuddered. Some of Fallon's nerves faded at the obvious proof of his desire. Apparently she wasn't the only one trembling with unfamiliar need. Cautiously, not sure exactly what he expected of her, she placed her hands on his shoulders. He was hard and strong, so powerful. Yet he held her and touched her as if she were a fragile and precious creature. He was a man of contrasts. A tough, successful businessman who hid the bruised soul of a poet.

He moved his head a little and pressed his mouth to the sensitive spot below her right ear. Tiny bolts of electricity raced through her as her breasts began to ache. Her legs trembled until she wondered if she could continue to stay upright. She leaned on him, letting his strength support her.

His tongue tasted her neck as he trailed a damp path to the hollow of her throat. Her breath caught there as sharp, exquisite desire grew.

"Jarrett," she whispered, because the sound of his name brought her pleasure.

"Tell me you want me," he commanded, his voice muffled as he moved lower, kissing her chest, then reaching the full curve of her breasts.

"I want you," she said easily, as if she'd spoken the words a thousand times before. As if this wasn't the first time they'd fallen from her lips. Perhaps it was easy because she'd wanted Jarrett for so long.

He dropped his hands to her bare shoulders and massaged her. He dipped down and licked the sensitive valley between her breasts. A thrill shot through her. The round flesh swelled more and she instinctively arched her back to give him more access. Her nipples were hard, tight buds. She wanted him to touch her there as he had a few nights before, only this time she didn't want the barrier of clothing between her hungry body and his hands.

He reached behind her and found the dress's zipper.

Long, lean fingers tugged it down. She felt the dress begin to slide to the ground.

Her first instinct was to grab it so she could cover herself. Then she reminded herself this was Jarrett. Not only did she want him, she trusted him. She let the garment slip over her hips before it pooled at her feet.

He raised his head and swore softly. The harsh word excited her as she caught the gleam of appreciation in his eyes. His dark gaze took in the strapless bra, her lace panties and the thigh-high stockings clinging to her legs.

She squared her shoulders, half proud, half nervous. She wanted him to want her. She wanted to reduce him to a quivering mass. The only problem was, she didn't know what to do with him when she got him that way. Pray God he could take charge.

Jarrett did. He gave her a smile that promised paradise, then bent and picked her up in his arms. Instinctively, she clung to him.

"My room is right here," she said.

"I know, but I've been dreaming about having you in *my* bed."

The possessiveness in his voice combined with the admission that he'd been thinking about them being together increased her nervousness. Maybe she should tell him the truth.

"Jarrett, I—"

He dropped his mouth to hers. Without thinking, she parted her lips and he swept inside.

His tongue stroked against hers. Heat flared between them. She could feel his hard chest against her side and the strength in his arms. Their breath mingled and she could not imagine a place she would rather be. It was as if she'd been born to be in his arms.

When he reached his room, he pushed the door open,

then kicked it shut behind him. Not breaking their kiss, he brushed against a light switch on the wall and a lamp came on in the corner. The faint illumination showed a large bed in the center of the room. Jarrett headed for that and placed her gently on the spread.

At last he released her mouth. "Second thoughts?" he asked. "I'll stop if you want me to."

Her senses were scattered, as if she'd been caught in a vortex of sensual pleasure. The world didn't spin exactly, but it wasn't as stable as she was used to. If this was passion, then that one taste had only whetted her appetite for more.

Stop? Why? "No second thoughts," she managed to say. She reached for his bow tie and pulled one end.

He grinned and shrugged out of his jacket. "Good. I would have stopped, but I would have been cranky as a bear."

"We can't have that," she said. "We must—"

He stopped her words with another kiss. As he teased her mouth, he lowered her onto the mattress. She relaxed beneath him, letting his broad chest shelter her.

There was much to explore, much to learn. She placed her fingers on his shoulders, then moved them lower across his back. Muscles bunched and released, rippling under her tentative touch. The contrast—his smooth, cool shirt, his hard, hot body—excited her.

One of his legs pressed possessively across hers. As her hand slipped lower, she felt the waistband of his trousers. Beyond that was the high, round swell of his buttocks. Hoping their deep kiss was enough to distract him, she boldly let her fingers trail along that curve.

Instantly his pelvis pressed into her. She felt something hard nestle against her hip. It was, she realized, the essence of his maleness—the proof of how much he wanted her.

"I wish you knew what you did to me," he told her as he slipped one hand behind her and unfastened her bra.

He worked the hooks expertly and drew the boned garment away. Before he touched her, he looked at her. "Beautiful," he whispered, and she felt that way. For now. For him.

He drew his hand around her rib cage then up higher to cup her bare breast. Her fingers curled into her palm. The heat between her thighs increased and she had the strongest urge to thrust toward him.

As his fingers circled her, moving closer to her taut peak, she found herself focusing completely on the perfect pleasure rippling through her. It was like heat with an edge. Tension increased and she found herself straining as if toward a goal.

At last he touched her nipple. He brushed the pad of his thumb against the tight tip. She bit her lower lip to keep from calling out. Her eyes drifted closed. He shifted, but she barely noticed. Then his mouth closed over her other breast.

Damp warmth caressed her. His tongue teased her. Forefinger and thumb matched the movements on her other breast. It was like a sensual dance, point and counterpoint, increasing her desire, like a wheel picking up speed on a steep hill. She couldn't speak, could barely breathe. There was only the man and the magic he created.

She didn't know she was making a sound until he lifted his head and smiled at her. "I love how you say my name."

"Am I?" She felt the heat on her cheeks.

"Like a prayer. Don't stop."

Don't stop. That's what she wanted to say to him. *Don't stop touching me this way. Don't stop making me feel these things.*

He read her mind. He returned his attention to her breasts, then one hand slipped lower, across her belly to the elastic edge of her panties. This time her hips did rise toward him, as if helping him achieve some goal that heretofore had been hidden from her.

When he tugged at the scrap of silk, she didn't protest. When he dropped his mouth from her breast to her rib cage, her whimper was barely audible. New pleasures distracted her.

He moved again, this time kneeling between her legs. He kissed her belly, then each hipbone. His hands rubbed up and down her thighs. With each sweep, his thumbs moved perilously close to her hot, damp center. Anticipation grew as did her restlessness. She wanted—she needed.

"Jarrett," she murmured.

"Soon," he promised.

Soon. Was he right? Would she finally experience all she'd read and heard about? Would the earth move and the heavens open? Did that really happen?

Before she could figure out a way to ask that question without sounding like a complete dork, he crouched down and pressed his tongue against her most secret place. The sensation was so amazing, so consuming, she didn't have heart or breath to protest. Instead, shameless and wanton, she dug her heels into the bed, raised her hips and pleaded, "Again."

He chuckled against her. "I thought you'd like that."

Like wasn't exactly the word she would have used. Adored. Loved. This feeling, the arousing, mind-numbing perfection that his tongue invoked was the stuff of dreams. She hadn't known feelings like this existed.

He explored and teased, then found a steady rhythm that caught her up in a journey from which there was no escape. She found herself panting and tensing, surging forward toward an unseen destination. He worked magic between her thighs, and as the pressure increased and she again called his name, he slipped one finger into her and stroked her from the inside.

The combination could not be survived. She exploded into starlight—shattered yet whole. In that space of time, with her body rippling and with Jarrett urging her to more and then more, she understood what it meant to love and be loved, why couples faced everything just to be together.

When the last ripple faded, she opened her eyes. Jarrett still knelt between her legs, watching her. His lips curled in a smile of pure male satisfaction.

"I'm impressed," he said.

"Me, too."

The smile faded as urgency took its place. She held open her arms. It was time. "Be with me," she told him.

Jarrett unbuttoned his shirt. Fallon wasn't going to have to ask him twice. He quickly shed his clothing, then reached for the protection in his nightstand drawer. As he slipped on the condom, she ran her hands over his chest.

"You're so beautiful," she said.

Her praise made him uncomfortable. "Guys aren't beautiful."

"Yes, they are." Her green eyes glittered. "I want you, Jarrett. I want you inside of me. I want you to be the one."

He almost asked her what she meant, but just as he

was about to, she parted her legs and gave a little thrust of her hips. It was all the encouragement he needed. He pressed against her tight opening, then slowly pushed inside.

The slight resistance didn't capture his attention in time. He was too busy gasping for breath at the wonder of her slick heat surrounding him. He tensed his muscles to plunge in deeper. Her arms wrapped around his shoulders and she gave a small moan of encouragement. He thrust into her, feeling a barrier stretch, then break.

Disbelief nearly surpassed desire. He glanced at her, not sure he understood what had just happened.

"Fallon?"

She bit her lower lip. "Don't stop, Jarrett. I want this. I want you."

I want you to be the one. Now he understood. The missing pieces fell into place. She was a virgin—or she *had* been. Not anymore, thanks to him.

Like the proof of her virginity, his conscience split in two. Even as he told himself to stop, to pull back, the entire essence of his being screamed at him to continue. He needed to be in her, with her. He needed them to be one.

And then it was too late to pull back. Her body's heated passage was too perfect, too tempting. He found himself moving in an age-old rhythm until there was no retreat. Until the ripple of her muscles around him drew him into paradise and he was left helpless as he spilled his seed and lost himself in pleasure.

When the last shudder had faded, he withdrew and sat on the edge of the bed. The enormity of what had just happened stunned him. What the hell had she been thinking?

"Jarrett?" Her voice was as tentative as the fingers tracing random patterns on his back. "Are you all right?"

"Isn't that my line?" he asked, wondering how something so wonderful could leave him feeling so bitter.

"I—I don't understand," she said. "I'm fine. Why wouldn't I be?"

He spun to face her. "You were a virgin."

A smile tugged at the corners of her mouth. "I know."

"You didn't tell me."

Her smile began to fade as confusion darkened her eyes. "Is it a problem? I guess I should have told you, but I didn't really think about it. I wanted us to make love." Confusion turned to shame. "It's because it wasn't very good, right? I mean, because I didn't know what to do? I'm sorry. I should have thought of that."

Her obvious pain left him feeling lower than sea slime. "It's not that," he muttered, wishing she *had* told him, because then he would have stopped. He would never have knowingly taken a virgin to his bed. He didn't want that—not the responsibility or the memories. He wanted to be able to walk away from her. He wanted this not to matter. She kept messing with his mind until it was going to be impossible for him to forget.

"Are you sure?" she asked

Of course he was sure. Being with her had been everything he'd wanted and more. For the first time in years he'd made love instead of having sex. He'd enjoyed more than his partner's body; he'd genuinely liked the person inside. He'd risked caring and had come out the loser, because he did care, damn her. He couldn't risk anything changing. His life was fine the way it was. He wouldn't do anything to recreate the past.

He drew his eyebrows together. "It's an old trick, Fal-

lon, and a good one. But it's not going to work on me.
I'm sorry you wasted yourself.''

He knew when she suddenly tried to cover her body
that his harsh words had struck at her heart. All the while
he'd loved her with his fingers and his tongue, she'd
never once thought about her nakedness. Now she
searched frantically for something to pull over herself.
He took pity on her and handed her his discarded shirt.

"What are you talking about?'' she asked, shrugging
into the garment and holding the front together. "What
trick?''

"You're trying to trap me.''

She flinched as if he'd slapped her. "How can you
think that? This wasn't a trap. I care about you. I thought
you cared, too. I thought—'' She closed her eyes. "I
thought you wanted me.''

He did, and that's what made it worse.

She opened her eyes and stared at him. "What went
wrong, Jarrett? What is so horrible that you have to pun-
ish me this way? I love you.''

Because she'd never lied before, he knew she spoke
the truth now. Her words were like a knife through his
flesh. They cut down to his heart, severing the organ and
leaving it in bloody pieces. He wanted to tell her he
didn't mean it. He wanted to reach out and hold her next
to him, begging her to say the words again and reassure
her with his own declarations.

He did nothing. He'd learned the risk of caring, of
trying to make something work. He knew the price of
being wrong.

She tossed her hair over her shoulder. "I never got it
before,'' she said. "I never understood about loving anyone. I thought I wasn't capable, or that I would be too

afraid. But I'm not. I love you, Jarrett. For the first time in my life I've been swept away. I'm not afraid.''

"I'd like you to leave."

Fallon told herself that he meant her to leave his bed, but in her soul she knew he meant this island—and his life. He didn't care that she loved him. For some reason, her precious gift had destroyed everything between them. Telling him she loved him had only made it worse. Perhaps she could understand if she knew why, but nothing made sense.

She'd offered him everything she had and he didn't want it. He didn't want her.

Her bedroom windows faced west, so she couldn't watch the sun rise. Instead the western sky lightened slowly, from black to gray to cream to blue. Her eyes felt gritty, her body ached. Some of the discomfort came from not having slept, but most of it was from the pain of loving Jarrett and having him reject her.

She continued to sit in the chair, watching the sky, waiting for time to pass. There was a plane leaving that morning and she would be on it. She'd already packed her bags. They waited by the bedroom door. Funny how quickly she'd been able to fold up her life to move on. If only she could neatly store away the memories. She would give anything to be able to forget again.

When she'd lost her memory, she hadn't appreciated the blessing not remembering could be.

She closed her eyes and, for the thousandth time, wondered what she'd done wrong. How had everything been destroyed? One minute he'd been touching her and showing her the magic possible between a man and a woman, the next he'd been accusing her of trying to trick him. It was as if he'd suddenly turned into a different man.

Fallon forced herself to take slow, shallow breaths. Telling herself she would recover didn't help. Probably because she recognized the lie for what it was. For the very first time in her life, she'd given her heart away. She'd trusted her very being with someone and he'd rejected her. In the space of a heartbeat, she'd both loved and lost. She'd been a fool to try.

But there was one thing she had to do before she left. One piece of business remained undone.

She rose to her feet and headed for the door. As she passed her dresser she saw the bottle sitting there—the one Anna Jane had used to send her note. She touched the cool glass. Tall, slender, beautiful. Perhaps in time she would regret leaving it behind, but right now she couldn't bear to look at it and remember the hope contained in a little girl's letter to a stranger—a letter that had stolen Fallon's heart. Who knew it was going to turn out like this?

She walked out into the hallway and moved quickly down the stairs. Jarrett's office door stood partially open. As she paused in front of it and gathered her courage, she felt his presence surround her. She wished it could have been different between them. She almost wished she could take back loving him. Almost. It might rip her apart. It might scar her for life, but it would never be wrong. Loving someone else was the purest human act. She was glad to have experienced it, however briefly.

She stepped inside. Jarrett sat facing the computer, his back to the door. She didn't announce herself; there was no point. He knew she was there. She saw it in the stiffening of his shoulders and back. Heard it in the sharp intake of air.

"I don't regret last night," she told him, proud of the fact that her voice didn't shake. "I wasn't trying to trick you into anything. Do you think because you took my virginity I expect you to marry me?''

He didn't answer and didn't turn around.

''I hadn't expected anything,'' she said. ''Except maybe that you would be willing to admit you enjoyed being with me. That, despite everything, you'd come to care about me.''

She swallowed against the pain building up inside her. Saying all this was harder than she'd thought, but she had to get the words out now before she lost control and broke down.

''I know how hard it is to trust love, to give of one's self,'' she told him. ''I know because I've been afraid, too. I watched what happened with my family, with my parents, and I swore nothing was going to hurt me that way again. I know my situation doesn't compare with what happened to you, but I do know what you're feeling.''

Silence. Damning silence. ''I hope that in time you can learn to let go of the past, Jarrett. I hope that you can love somebody enough to trust them with your heart. You deserve that. As for me, I suppose I'll always love you. My sisters have only ever loved one man each and I'm exactly like them. I don't think we know how to be any other way.''

Her throat tightened. ''I suppose that's what I regret the most. That we could have had the same kind of relationship my sisters have with their husbands. I've envied them that. If only—''

She gave a half laugh, half sob. ''If only. Isn't that the stupidest expression you've ever heard? If only doesn't change a thing. I thought we could be like them. I thought anyone would be thrilled to have a chance at that. Obviously I was wrong.''

She drew in a deep breath and laced her fingers together in front of her waist. "Jarrett, I want your permission to take Anna Jane with me. I'm a teacher and I understand her needs. I would love her and care for her as if she were my own child. That way you wouldn't have to worry about her."

He hit several keys on his computer, then slowly turned to face her. The expressionless stranger she remembered from the early days of her visit had returned. His gaze gave nothing away.

"No," he said harshly. "Anna Jane stays with me."

"What are you going to do with her? You can't leave her trapped here on this island, and it's not a good idea to send her to boarding school. She would feel completely abandoned."

"You're right," he agreed. "I'm going to be moving back to the States. That way she can live with me and go to a normal school with other children."

She felt as if he'd slapped her. He wasn't willing to trust her, Fallon, with having given herself to him because she cared, but he was willing to leave his prison for the sake of Anna Jane. It would have been better if she'd never known that. At least then she could have fooled herself into thinking he wasn't capable of loving anyone. Now that she knew he loved his niece, she realized he simply chose not to love *her*.

She searched for something to say, some final words of parting that would make him remember her with fondness or at least dignity. There were none. Instead of speaking, she backed out of the room, then turned on her heel and ran upstairs where she could lick her wounds in private.

* * *

The whine of the jet made it difficult to talk, as did the tears and the rawness of her throat.

"I'm going to miss you," she said, holding the child close to her.

"Me, too," Anna Jane responded, then sobbed. "Every single day. Fallon, I don't want you to go."

"I know." The gravel bit into her knees, but Fallon didn't move. Nothing mattered but this sweet child. "I don't want to go, either, but I have to. It's the right thing to do."

"Why?"

The child's cry came from her heart. Fallon winced. "It's too hard to explain."

"Don't you love me and Uncle Jarrett?"

"With all my heart. But sometimes loving someone isn't enough."

"Uncle Jarrett loves you back. Isn't that enough?"

It would be if he did. But he didn't, and she couldn't make him.

"I'll write you," she promised. "When you move back to the mainland, you tell me your new address and I'll make sure we stay in touch. Maybe I'll come visit."

Anna Jane hugged her tighter. "Promise. Promise me you'll come visit and that you won't forget me."

Tears burned down her cheeks. Fallon hadn't known there was this much pain in the world.

"I promise," she whispered.

Chapter Sixteen

Anna Jane tightened her hold on her mermaid pendant, but it wasn't helping. She swallowed hard, but the lump in her throat wouldn't go away. It was warm, bright and sunny yet she felt cold inside. Cold and empty. Fallon had been gone for a week and nothing was the same anymore.

She curled up in the lounge chair by the pool and stared at her uncle's office. Since Fallon had left, he'd been in there all the time. A few days ago she'd asked him why. He'd said something about having to catch up, but she didn't believe him anymore. Uncle Jarrett might not want to admit it to anyone, but he missed Fallon as much as she did.

From here Anna Jane could see her uncle's desk and his bent shoulders. He didn't stand very straight anymore. She'd noticed he wasn't eating his dinner and at night sometimes she heard him pacing through the house. Her mom had been like this when her father had died. At least Uncle Jarrett remembered to notice her and speak to her, although not the way he had before. But he was still reading her stories at night and that was nice.

Anna Jane rubbed her thumb across the mermaid's body. "Tell me what to do," she whispered fiercely. "Tell me how to make it better."

What was the answer? Should she talk to Uncle Jarrett? Should she send another note in her bottle?

Anna Jane frowned. She didn't want a new friend, she wanted Fallon back. A note wasn't going to help. Maybe she could call her and ask her to come home. Only, something was wrong between Uncle Jarrett and Fallon. Anna Jane sensed deep in her heart that until whatever it was between them had been fixed, Fallon wasn't going to return. At least, not anytime soon.

So she, Anna Jane, was going to have to figure out what was wrong and then make it better. Resolved, she got to her feet and walked into the house. As she approached her uncle's office, she raised her head and squared her shoulders. She would make him listen to her. She would make him see that everything was better with Fallon around.

But as she stepped inside, she saw that he wasn't even pretending to work. He was just staring into space. She wondered if he would hear her if she called his name.

Before she could say anything, he got all stiff, then his face scrunched up as if he were going to cry. The thought of her uncle breaking down was too frightening. With a muffled sob of her own, she raced from the room and started up the stairs. As she climbed, she felt something cold slipping down her spine. The creatures under the stairs were back.

* * *

The Grand Cayman Islands were as beautiful as the cruise brochure had promised and Fallon couldn't have cared less. She sat in the bus trying to feign enthusiasm and failing badly. The older lady sitting next to her on the tour bus kept asking if she was all right. Fallon would nod and say she was a little tired. At least that much was true. She was dead tired. She hadn't slept well since leaving St. Alicia.

After spending three days in Miami, she'd been able to get a last-minute cabin on a cruise ship heading for two weeks into the Caribbean. A quick phone call to her sisters had informed them of her travel plans, but she'd hung up before they could ask any questions. Obviously they wanted to know why she'd left Jarrett's so abruptly. They were her family and an intimate part of her life. Eventually she would come clean with them. But not yet. Not when the humiliation and pain were so fresh.

The bus stopped in front of a tiny house built entirely of shells. Her fellow passengers crowded on her side of the bus to take pictures. She obligingly ducked out of the way and wished she was more excited about this trip. A couple of months ago she would have been having the time of her life. Now nothing mattered.

Snap out of it, she told herself firmly. She couldn't go on like this forever. Eventually she was going to have to pick up the pieces and move on.

But it was so hard. Not a moment went by without her remembering and missing both Jarrett and Anna Jane. That made it worse. She could have survived missing just one of them, but both—that was impossible.

She'd already written to Anna Jane twice. With any luck the child would have written back. It wasn't much and it certainly wasn't the same as being with her, but it would have to do. It was more than she had with Jarrett.

The bus tour continued. They made a stop in Hell, a tiny post office on the edge of a volcano crater. Tourists bought postcards to have them postmarked in Hell. Fallon strolled around, ignoring the souvenirs and the other passengers. Despite the people around her, she'd never felt so alone. She missed Anna Jane's hugs, her humor and her sweetness. She missed Jarrett's laughter, his touch, everything about him. She wanted him in her life, but he didn't want her. Where did that leave her?

As she sat on a stone bench and wondered how long she was going to feel this badly, she consoled herself with the fact that at least she'd tried. For once in her life she'd given with a full heart. No matter what else happened, she would always know that she'd had the courage of her convictions. She'd loved fully.

Eventually she would be able to function without thinking about him. There was a whole world waiting for her out there. She would survive being alone because there wasn't another choice.

Until his world returned to black and white, Jarrett hadn't realized he'd grown used to the color. The house was a prison, and even though he planned to escape, he had a feeling the cold grayness would follow wherever he went.

He tapped a few keys on his computer, then leaned back in his chair and gave up the pretense of working. Nothing mattered anymore. There was a deal going bad in Hong Kong and he couldn't make himself care.

He'd let her go. There was no other way to describe what had happened. Fallon had come willingly to his bed, given her most precious gift and he'd tossed her aside. Because of the fear. Because no matter how much he wanted her, he was terrified of the past repeating itself.

He didn't want to be responsible for something horrible happening to her.

Charlotte's death had been senseless and tragic, but he'd never loved the woman. He blamed himself, and had retreated from the world, vowing never to risk that again. Until now, he'd been fine. He'd adjusted to being alone— an easy adjustment, because he'd always lived cut off from what most people considered normal. Until a mysterious stranger had crept into view. Until soft laughter and a gentle soul had found a place inside him. Until he'd learned what it was like to want to love someone.

Soft footsteps caught his attention. He turned in his chair and saw Anna Jane approaching. The pain in her eyes matched that in his own. She easily showed what he kept inside. They were both suffering, and he didn't know how to make it better.

He opened his arms to her. She climbed onto his lap. "I have something to show you," she said, and held up a small package.

He pressed his lips together to hold back a wince. He knew what she'd picked up at the hotel that morning— the pictures she'd taken during the holidays. Pictures of Fallon and her family.

"Want to see?" she asked.

He nodded, because it was the answer she wanted to hear. Fallon was her friend and someone she missed. Talking about her made things easier for Anna Jane. He would pay whatever price necessary to make up for bringing more tragedy to the child's life.

She pulled out the pictures. The first one showed Kayla and Elissa laughing together. There were shots of the sisters with their husbands, of Fallon with her sisters, of Anna Jane with each of the women. Everyone was smiling and laughing. Without wanting to, he remembered that morning, and his own lips turned up briefly. It had been the best Christmas ever.

Anna Jane went through them slowly, showing each to him, telling him what she liked and didn't like. He absorbed the images and felt the hole inside him grow wider and deeper. At one time he'd thought he would be doing Fallon a favor by "allowing" her to spend time with him and Anna Jane. In the end, she'd been the one doing them a favor. She'd opened her heart and given all that she had.

Anna Jane flipped to another picture. His body froze. He and Fallon sat together on the sofa. He was listening to someone offscreen, but she was staring at him. The love on her face was so powerful, even he recognized it.

"Mommy used to look at Daddy like that," Anna Jane said softly.

"I know," he replied, his throat tight.

"Fallon loves you, Uncle Jarrett. Did that make you mad?"

"No." Far from it. He'd been honored by her love.

Then why the hell did you send her away? The voice screamed inside his head. He had no answer.

"When I talked to Fallon about loving Nana B. more than Mommy she told me it was okay to love more than one person. She said it's never wrong to love someone. And it's never wrong to miss them, either."

Anna Jane put the pictures on the desk and looked at him. "I'm scared, Uncle Jarrett. I'm scared 'cause Fallon went away. I don't want you to go away, too."

"I'm not going anywhere," he promised. "Leona is packing so you and I can go to New York together. You're going to go to school during the day and come home to me at night. I'll always be there. I promise."

Her gaze never left his. He hadn't convinced her. "I

love you, Anna Jane. You're a wonderful girl and I'm lucky to have you in my life."

"But what if you don't want me anymore? You thought Fallon was wonderful, and she's gone."

"I was a fool."

He spoke without thinking, then realized it was true.

She frowned. "I don't understand."

"I was afraid. I was afraid to love her the way your mother loved your father, or the way Charlotte loved me."

"Who's Charlotte?"

"No one you know. I can't explain it, except that when you're grown up, it can be easy not to love people."

"Then they don't love you back."

The simple truth of a child. "I know."

"But Fallon loves you back. You shouldn't have let her go."

He'd been afraid. It all came down to trusting himself enough to let himself risk it all.

He'd been so quick to accuse her, because people wanting something was all he understood. But Fallon wasn't like that. She gave, expecting nothing in return. All she'd needed was for him to accept her gift and love her back. Was he so much of a shell he couldn't even offer her that?

"What have I done?" he asked.

"You were very wrong," Anna Jane told him. "Now you're going to have to win her back. It's not that hard. Princes have to win back their princesses all the time. You have to tell her you love her and then ask her to marry you." She lowered her voice confidentially. "Ladies like the marriage part very much."

He hugged her tight. "When did you get to be so smart?"

"I've always been smart." She fumbled with her necklace. "I want to give you the mermaid. For luck."

He kissed her cheek. "How about I take you with me and you can give me luck in person?"

"Really?"

He nodded.

"Uncle Jarrett, I love you the best of everyone."

It was the last formal night of the cruise. Fallon smiled and made polite conversation at the dinner table. She was sure her fellow passengers were sick and tired of her long face and would be happy to see the last of her. She tried to pretend to be happy, but she'd never been much good at lying.

Without meaning to, she reached up and fingered the gold mermaid enhancer resting on her pearls. The lady next to her leaned close.

"I've been admiring your necklace all night. It's very beautiful."

"Thank you. It was a Christmas gift."

The woman smiled. "Obviously from an admirer."

Fallon forced herself to nod pleasantly. "Yes. He was very thoughtful." Right up to the time he ripped her heart out and danced on it.

She tried to work up a little righteous indignation, but all she could do was wonder where he was right now. What was he doing? Was he thinking of her? How was Anna Jane?

The waiter moved in her direction. She picked up her menu and tried to focus on the words. She wasn't hungry. She didn't think she could choke her way through another meal. Maybe she should just return to her cabin and stop trying to fake it. Maybe a night of good old-fashioned tears would help her start healing.

She closed the menu. "I'm not very hungry."

"Good, because I'm not ready to take your order. I have a gift." He motioned to his left and one of the other waiters brought her a large glass bottle.

Fallon stared unbelievingly. The elegant container was a series of bubbles sitting on top of each other, larger at the base, smaller at the top. She recognized the bottle.

Afraid to look around and find out she was completely wrong, she took the bottle and uncorked it. There was a note inside.

The passengers at her table noticed what was happening and looked at her.

"What is it?" the woman next to her asked.

"I'm not sure." Her fingers were shaking so hard, it was difficult to unfold the paper. Finally she got it open and began to read.

My name is Jarrett Wilkenson and I'm thirty-two years old. I live in a big house on an island. If you find this note, I hope you'll forgive me for being a fool. I love you and need you in my life. Please be my friend, my lover, my wife. Please tell me it's not too late.

Fallon looked up and saw Jarrett standing a few feet away. He was male elegance at its finest in his black tux and starched white shirt. Anna Jane stood next to him. Her emerald green dress emphasized her dark hair and eyes. The girl was grinning madly and waving, but it was the painful longing in Jarrett's expression that caught Fallon's attention.

He moved toward her and dropped to one knee. "I'm so sorry," he said, taking both her hands in his. "I was afraid of loving you because I thought love meant pain.

But pain is being away from you. You are the best part of me. You bring color to my life. I can't imagine a world without you." His dark eyes gleamed with the fires of love. "I have nothing to offer. You already have a family and money."

She smiled. "I think your fortune is a little bigger."

"That's not enough," he said. "Tell me you'll forgive me. Please give me another chance. I'll do anything, say anything. Marry me."

She flung herself at him, wrapping her arms around his shoulders. "I love you, Jarrett. I understand about being afraid and alone. I don't care about the rest of it."

"So you'll marry me?"

She nodded. "Yes. I want to be with you always. I want to raise Anna Jane as our own and maybe have a couple of kids to keep her company."

He squeezed her tighter. "Thank you. I swear you won't regret it."

She straightened and he kissed her. As her eyes drifted closed she noticed that Anna Jane had moved closer and was taking their picture with a disposable camera. Around them came the whirring sound that warned her she and Jarrett were about to become featured players in several home videos.

"This kiss is going to make us famous," she murmured.

"I don't do anything by halves."

His lips touched hers again and she knew he was right. When Jarrett made up his mind, there was no stopping him. She would have a lifetime of loving with this man. They would conquer the demons from the past and find perfect happiness—together.

Epilogue

Seven years later

The director was a tall, thin man who kept talking about wanting to get at the "essence" of the original show.

"It's been twenty years," Kayla said from her seat. "That's some pretty old essence."

Elissa bit back a giggle. Trying not to break into laughter herself, Fallon glared at her sister. "You're being impossible."

Mrs. Beecham, a little grayer, a little more frail, beamed at them. "I'm so impressed with you three. You've turned out to be spectacular adults. You're successful and have wonderful families."

"We owe that all to you," Kayla told the woman. They sat in a half circle in front of several television cameras in a Los Angeles studio. "I still remember you telling us love was like a tornado and we weren't to settle for anything else.''

Mrs. Beecham frowned. "What on earth are you talking about?''

Elissa looked at her. "You always said that. To make sure we really care about the man, we should feel a storm of passion. Like a tornado.''

Mrs. Beecham chuckled. "Nonsense. And you girls listened to me?''

"Of course," Fallon said. "It's turned out great.''

"Ladies?" the director called. "Let's try this again. From the top, please.''

"Quiet!" a voice ordered loudly.

Fallon waited until the marker had snapped, then she looked directly at the camera in front of her and smiled. "Good evening, and welcome to the twentieth anniversary of 'The Sally McGuire Show.' Don't try adjusting your set. You're not really seeing—'' she glanced at her sisters for a second "—triple. There were three of us playing that wonderful character we remember so well.''

Elissa picked up the dialogue and explained who they were and how they'd come to be on the show. Kayla continued with a brief recap of where each of them were now.

"Fallon and I each have twin boys," Kayla said, "while Elissa has triplet girls.''

Fallon turned to her left. Just off the set, their families waited. Fathers held babies, while Anna Jane took care of the older children. Her own five-year-old twins were more than a handful, and next to Jarrett and Anna Jane, they were the greatest source of joy in her life. She knew her sisters felt the same way about their children.

Maybe Mrs. Beecham hadn't realized what she'd been saying when she'd talked about love being a tornado, but the advice had been sound. Each of the sisters had found happiness through a marriage that was a living testament to their heartfelt belief that love was the greatest blessing of all.

* * * * *

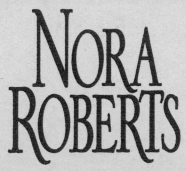

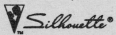

Take 4 bestselling love stories FREE

Plus get a FREE surprise gift!

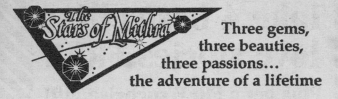

The Stars of Mithra

Three gems,
three beauties,
three passions...
the adventure of a lifetime

SILHOUETTE·INTIMATE·MOMENTS®
brings you a thrilling new series by
New York Times bestselling author

Nora Roberts

Three mystical blue diamonds place three close
friends in jeopardy...and lead them to romance.

In October
HIDDEN STAR (IM#811)
Bailey James can't remember a thing, but she knows
she's in big trouble. And she desperately needs private
investigator Cade Parris to help her live long enough to
find out just what kind.

In December
CAPTIVE STAR (IM#823)
Cynical bounty hunter Jack Dakota and spitfire
M. J. O'Leary are handcuffed together and on the run
from a pair of hired killers. And Jack wants to know
why—but M.J.'s not talking.

In February
SECRET STAR (IM#835)
Lieutenant Seth Buchanan's murder investigation takes
a strange turn when Grace Fontaine turns up alive. But
as the mystery unfolds, he soon discovers the notorious
heiress is the biggest mystery of all.

Available at your favorite retail outlet.

SILHOUETTE WOMEN KNOW ROMANCE WHEN THEY SEE IT.

And they'll see it on **ROMANCE CLASSICS**, the new 24-hour TV channel devoted to romantic movies and original programs like the special **Romantically Speaking—Harlequin™ Goes Prime Time.**

Romantically Speaking—Harlequin™ Goes Prime Time introduces you to many of your favorite romance authors in a program developed exclusively for Harlequin® and Silhouette® readers.

Watch for **Romantically Speaking—Harlequin™ Goes Prime Time** beginning in the summer of 1997.

If you're not receiving ROMANCE CLASSICS, call your local cable operator or satellite provider and ask for it today!

ROMANCE CLASSICS

Escape to the network of your dreams.

See Ingrid Bergman and Gregory Peck in *Spellbound* on Romance Classics.

Share in the joy of yuletide romance with brand-new
stories by two of the genre's most beloved writers

DIANA PALMER
and
JOAN JOHNSTON
in

LONE STAR
CHRISTMAS

Diana Palmer and Joan Johnston share their favorite
Christmas anecdotes and personal stories in this
special hardbound edition.

Diana Palmer delivers an irresistible spin-off of her
LONG, TALL TEXANS series and Joan Johnston crafts an
unforgettable new chapter to **HAWK'S WAY** in this wonderful
keepsake edition celebrating the holiday season. So
perfect for gift giving, you'll want one for yourself...and
one to give to a special friend!

Available in November at your favorite retail outlet!

Only from
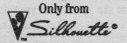
Silhouette®